A Slice OF LOVE

TEAGAN HUNTER

Editing by Editing by C. Marie
Cover Image from iStock
Formatting by AB Formatting

JONAS

FOUR YEARS AGO

The last time I was this nervous was freshman year when I stepped onto the football field for the first time as a varsity player.

I didn't realize it then, but my life was about to change.

Everything, not just football.

The person I was expected to become changed overnight. The people I was supposed to interact with shifted on a major scale. The standards that had been set were obliterated, all new ones put in place. And the rumors that had never breathed life before suddenly had all the oxygen they'd ever need to survive.

Everything was different after that first Friday night.

I was different.

As I stand here on the doorstep of the only person in my life who knows me as Jonas Schwartz and not Jonas Schwartz *the quarterback,* this moment is just as big as that first foot I let fall onto the field.

Everything is going to change again.

I don't know how I know; I just do.

Or it's wishful thinking.

Either way, I'm here, and I'm not going to miss whatever this is…or what it will become.

Lifting my hand, I rap my knuckles against the deep blue door.

Quickly, before she can answer, I wipe my sweaty palms on my jeans.

Sweaty palms? Seriously? Get a fucking grip, Jonas. You've faced much bigger obstacles than this on the field.

But that's just it—those obstacles were on the field.

Spending an entire weekend with my crush and trying to keep my hands off her because she's the daughter of two very prominent people in our town? Well, a game against our biggest rival ain't shit compared to this.

I hear scuttling from behind the door.

Yet nothing happens.

I'm almost certain *she* is standing on the other side.

I picture her mess of red frizz being tousled more than usual because she can't stop running her hands through it, the nerves getting the better of her.

I bet she has her thick bottom lip crushed between her teeth, bet she can't seem to stop herself from chewing on it despite the fact that it's splitting and cracking and has to be painful at this point.

I imagine her fingers are pulling at the hem of that black cardigan she's always wearing.

There's no doubt in my mind she's every bit as nervous as I am, maybe even more.

She's the town good girl, and when it comes to me, good is a word they only use to describe my playing abilities.

She's completely off limits.

Sucks for me because I've been crushing on Frankie Callahan for years now. Which is why when we were *finally* seated next to one another for the first time during our high school careers, I took advantage of it.

I slid a notebook her way with a silly message in it.

She sent something back.

We've been thick as thieves since. Not that I'd admit it to anyone, but hell, she's probably my best friend based on everything she knows about me. That's damn insane considering we've only spoken to one another aloud a handful of times.

But that's what college will be for.

With the school year winding down, it's almost all our notes have been about—our escape route. She's going for some bullshit degree her parents want her to get. I'm headed there for football.

None of that matters though. The point is we'll be there together. Just us.

We'll be free there, and I can't fucking wait.

The lock slides, signaling she's *finally* going to open the door, and I exhale a heavy breath to steady myself.

Fuck. Here we go.

She pulls the door open with such slowness it's almost painful to watch.

When her face finally appears in the opening, I can't help but smile, because that damn bottom lip *is* tucked tightly between her teeth.

"Hey, Frank," I say.

Her eyes widen, like she wasn't expecting me to be real.

That familiar color of blush steals up her cheeks when she realizes I've gone and called her Frank again.

"Jonas."

7

She says my name on a quiet breath but makes no move to let me in. I *need* her to let me in, not because I can't wait to get this weekend started, but because the longer I linger on her front porch, the more likely it is someone will spot me, and the jig will be up.

I'm aware that what we're doing, me sneaking over to her house for the weekend while her parents are away is wrong, but I don't care.

I want this too much. I want to spend time with her without the prying eyes. I want to get to know her.

"I told you, it's Frankie," she murmurs shyly, because that's exactly what she is—shy.

It's a reason we'd make no sense together.

Frankie Callahan is everything I'm not.

She's the golden girl. Untouchable. She's perfect.

It's not that I'm a bad guy. I respect my teachers and parents and I get good grades. And even though I do all of those things and I lead the football team, I'm nowhere near good enough for her.

"I thought we agreed Frank suits you better."

"No, *you* decided it did."

"I don't think I heard you argue when I said it. You just blushed." I grin at her and watch as her cheeks deepen in color. "Like you are now."

She shoves at the big, bulky glasses she always wears and pulls on the frayed edge of her sweater again. It's the same one she wears to school every day.

She still doesn't invite me in, and I can feel myself start to fidget because standing out in the open is beginning to make me nervous.

A sure sign you're about to fuck up, Jonas. Walk away now.

Walk away.

It's exactly what I *should* do.

Instead I hear myself say, "So, Frank, you gonna make me do our project from the porch?"

8

Her brown eyes widen, and she lets out a tiny squeak. "Right, right." She pulls the door open wider. "Come in, please."

Frankie moves aside and I squeeze past. I'm dying to touch her, even in the smallest way, but I'm careful not to brush against her.

My chest tightens when I step across the threshold and into the dark, quiet home.

It's cold in here, and I don't mean temperature-wise.

You can *feel* the lack of love in this place.

Because of the notebooks we've been passing back and forth all year long, I know that's because of Frankie's parents.

They're not exactly…welcoming.

They're not awful, but they don't allow her to be…well, *her*.

It's their way. Always.

They love her on some level, but at the same time, they don't *know* her.

Not like I do.

They don't know that she loves to draw because she has to hide her notebooks. They have no clue that her favorite kind of candy is chocolate-covered raisins because she's not allowed to have candy. And they would be lost if they ever had to pick her favorite musical artist out of a lineup because they don't know it's the Rolling Stones and not the worship music they constantly play.

They might actually talk to her, but sometimes written words speak a whole hell of a lot louder than spoken ones.

"Your house is…"

"Cold? Lonely? Empty? Draining?" she says with a lifted brow.

I laugh lightly. "I was going to say lovely, but you took a more honest approach."

She lifts a shoulder. "It's true. It's why I don't ever invite anyone over." She purses her lips. "Well, that and I don't have any friends."

Her big eyes fill to the brim with sadness, and I hate that the tightness in my chest is no longer because of the cold but because of the loneliness in her gaze—and because of the realization that she doesn't consider *us* friends.

Though I suppose that's fair.

"You have friends, Frank," I say anyway, trying to get her to see that, even though I can't show it, I do care about her.

"Yeah? You see me sit with them often in the cafeteria?"

I shove my hands in my pockets to keep from reaching out and pulling her into my arms where I can wrap her up tightly and protect her from everything and everyone. "I'd sit with you."

"But you can't."

My shoulders droop and I nod. "Right. I can't."

She doesn't say anything, just looks up at me with that same lonely stare.

"But I want to."

Her breath stutters just a bit, and she darts her tongue out to wet her lips as they drop open.

She looks like she wants to say something else, but she doesn't. Instead her full lips curve into a smile. "Want a snack?"

God, she sounds like an after-school special right now.

"Sure. A snack would be nice."

And I sound like a fucking moron.

I follow her into the kitchen, hot on her heels but not close enough to touch because I'm not a fucking masochist.

Or maybe I am.

I mean, I *am* here to spend an entire weekend with her, after all.

I could kiss my chemistry teacher right now for seating us beside each other on that first day of school. It got us here, gave me my in.

Now here we are.

Me and Frankie. A whole fucking weekend together.

No teachers. No parents. No prying eyes.

We can talk. We can laugh. We can do *anything* we want and nobody is going to be there to judge or report.

Just us.

It makes me nervous, yet so damn excited I can barely stand it.

I try to play it cool as we move through her oversized house. I know it's just Frankie and her parents, but somehow their house is nearly three times as big as the one my family of four lives in.

She's on the north side of the island with all the other well-off folks in this town.

Me? Well, my dad may run a successful business, but I definitely *do not* live on the north end.

We enter the sprawling kitchen, and the first thing I spy is a plethora of snacks lining the counter. There are at least six different bags of chips, a couple boxes of crackers, and a few two-liters of soda.

"You planning on having a party or something, Frank? That's a whole lot of food for two."

Her eyes dart toward the haul of goodies and then back to me. Her brown orbs track over my body, darkening in their perusal.

If I'm not mistaken, that's lust in her gaze.

"You're a growing boy."

I quirk a brow at her. "Are you saying you've noticed my body?"

She drops her head, hiding behind that mess of frizz. "N-N-No."

I love how easily embarrassed she is.

Chuckling, I cross the room until I'm standing just a foot away from her.

She doesn't move. Doesn't look up.

I let my eyes roam over her. She's petite compared to my large frame. I bet we look ridiculous standing next to each other with how small she is compared to me.

Her red locks are wild as usual, and her oversized glasses are slowly sliding down her nose like they always do. With her cardigan covering her shoulders and her blue jeans hugging her curves, she looks just like she does at school. Well, minus being barefoot, and I won't even get into how adorable I find her blue-painted toes.

Frankie's cute as fuck, and she doesn't even realize it.

I slide my finger under her chin, tilting her face up until she's looking at me. Her lips part when her eyes meet mine, her chest now moving up and down as her breathing picks up in response to our proximity—or maybe it's me touching her so freely that's affecting her.

I don't know why I have my hands on her. They don't belong there.

Then why does it feel so right?

"It's okay, Frank. I've noticed your body too."

A soft gasp leaves her lips, and she takes a step toward me, leaving mere inches separating us.

I know if I closed the gap, she'd fall against me.

She'd *beg* me to kiss her.

And I want to kiss her so fucking bad.

Her eyes fall shut. "J-Jonas…"

"Yeah, Frank?"

Her tongue darts out to wet her lips again. "What kind of chips do you want?"

I've been inside Frankie's house for six hours now, and we haven't moved from the kitchen since I came back inside with my backpack.

"Where's your stuff for the project?"

"In my car."

"That's not very helpful, Jonas."

"Yeah, well, I wasn't sure you were going to let me in."

She just nodded, like *she* hadn't been sure she'd let me in either.

We've been planted at the kitchen counter since. There's glue and scissors and poster board and two half-eaten bags of chips spread out in front of us.

"I think we're almost done," Frankie comments, letting her eyes dance over the mess we've made. She pops another chip into her mouth, moaning at the flavor exploding on her tongue.

From our notebooks, I know she's not allowed to have junk food like this in the house, which makes the little noises she keeps making all that more adorable.

"Already?"

"Yep." She nods. "We make a pretty good team."

"We do, huh?"

She blushes, and I bump my shoulder with hers.

"So, Frank," I start as I rock my stool back until it's balancing on two legs. "Since we're already done with this project that was supposed to take us two days, whatever will we do with the rest of the weekend?"

"Well, Jonas, for starters, you're going to put your chair down on all fours." She narrows her eyes at me.

I let the stool fall back to the floor. "Done. Now what?"

"We're going to finish the project. I didn't say we were done. I said we're *almost* done."

"Almost done is practically done."

"Is that so?"

"It is." I nod. "Let's take a break."

"A break? Why? We're close to being finished."

"Do you *really* want to finish this *right now* and then have nothing at all to do the rest of the weekend but think about how badly you want me to kiss you?"

She lets out a low squeak and almost topples off her stool in surprise.

Feeling like Edward Cullen when he races after Bella—damn my sister and all those girly movies she forced me to watch—I catch her just before she hits the ground.

"Jesus, Frank," I say, hands gripped tightly around her biceps, righting her.

"Don't you 'Jesus' me, Jonas Schwartz!" In a surprising move, she swats at me. "You can't just say things like that!"

"Say that again."

"Say what again? You can't just—"

"Not that part," I interrupt. "My name. Say my name again."

"Jonas."

"My full name," I demand, my breaths coming just as sharp as hers, and she's the one who almost fell off her stool. I'm sure I sound like a damn idiot right now, but I don't care. My name falling from her lips is a dream come fucking true. "Please."

Her chestnut eyes bore into me, her pupils growing twice their size.

"Jonas Schwartz."

She whispers it, calmly.

Certainly.

And I want to fucking break.

I want to erase every single stupid invisible line we've drawn between us and haul her against me and *finally* kiss her like I've been dying to since freshman year.

I want to so goddamn badly.

But I don't.

With a sigh, I drag her closer, dropping my forehead against hers.

"Fuck, Frank. You can't just say things like that."

I hear her swallow thickly, can feel her shaking as she reaches up, placing her hands on my forearms.

Her fingers curl into me as she pulls herself closer.

She's so close now I can feel her ragged breaths on my lips.

"Jonas."

Now I'm the one swallowing thickly.

"Frank."

Her fingers squeeze me once. Twice. She moves even closer. Then I feel it—her lips against mine.

Her touch is light. Cautious. I can feel the spot where she always bites down and chews. It's rough and torn, but I don't care.

Frankie is kissing me.

Frankie is fucking kissing *me*.

Although everything inside me is screaming for more, I don't dare move, too worried I'll scare her away and this will end just as fast as it began—and that's the last thing I want.

She brushes her lips against mine again. And again.

I'm dying, just fucking *dying* under her slow, gentle assault.

Then, all too soon, she pulls away.

I exhale a heavy, almost relieved breath, because if she had left her lips against mine for just one more second…

"Jonas." She says my name again, the single word uttered with a force of need. I don't think she even realizes how she sounds right now, how scratchy and hoarse her voice is coming out.

I peel my eyes open, looking down at her, trying hard to mask the lust in them.

She's peering up at me with a heavy gaze that's asking if she can do it again.

Again? Try always.

I bend until we're eye level so I can hold her brown eyes with my green ones.

Reaching out, I slide my hand up her cheek and into her red frizz, rubbing the strands between my fingers like I've always wanted to do.

They feel like silk between the pads of my fingertips. I don't ever want to let them go.

She leans into my touch, enjoying it just as much as I am.

With the fingers of my free hand, I trace her thick bottom lip, wanting so badly to feel it against mine again. Her exhalations ghost along the tips, and I can feel the way her breaths have picked up yet again.

Chest heaving, she's gazing at me expectedly. Like she's waiting for me to capture her lips with mine.

And I want to. So damn badly.

But I can't take it. It has to be her decision.

I decided that the day I agreed to her crazy idea of us spending the weekend together.

If Frankie asks me to kiss her, I will. But I won't take what isn't mine.

She has to offer.

"I'll only kiss you if you ask me to, Frank."

Slice Two

FRANKIE

I blink up at him.

I'll only kiss you if you ask me to, Frank.

God, do I want him to.

No, not want—*need*.

I *need* Jonas Schwartz to kiss me.

To press his lips against mine. To make my world shift.

Because that's what will happen the moment he kisses me. I know with every fiber of my being I will never, ever be the same again.

Which sounds incredibly stupid since we've hardly ever spoken to one another. It's not for lack of wanting to. We simply can't.

Jonas is…well, Jonas. He's the quarterback of our championship-winning football team. He's Mister Popular with all the typical things that come along with it—girls, parties, and mischief. He has that *it* factor, and he uses it to his advantage plenty. He's untouchable.

I'm untouchable in other ways. My father is the town pastor, and my mother the principal. I'm Miss Perfect…but not in a good way. Everyone avoids me like the plague. We live in a small community; rumors already run rampant. Getting involved with the daughter of two of the most influential people in town? Not going to happen. Fear keeps everyone away.

Somehow, though, we found a way to break through our social statuses this year. Turns out we don't need spoken words to get to know each other.

No. Our secrets are bled into the pages of a cheap notebook, making them lasting…binding.

Ours.

Nobody else. Just us.

Which is why I *need* Jonas to kiss me.

Now.

I've been waiting to feel his mouth on me for months.

"Will you kiss m—?"

The last word isn't even out of my mouth before his lips are covering mine. His hot, hard mouth is pressing firm against my own. I don't know anything about kisses because this is my first, but I'd dare to say he's kissing me like he's hungry and will never be satisfied again.

His touch is soft yet hard, primal but restrained.

He wants more.

I want more.

Like he can read my thoughts, he pulls away.

He rests his forehead against mine, his harsh breaths making his chest pump up and down in rapid succession.

"Frank, this weekend…" He swallows hard. "*This* isn't what this is about. I'm just here for the project, to hang out with you without everyone staring at us like we don't belong together. I'm not here for anything else. I'm not trying to pressure you into anything. I just—"

"Jonas?" I interrupt.

Another swallow. "Yeah?"

"Just kiss me again. If anything is too much, I'll tell you. I just want you to kiss me like you've always wanted to kiss me."

He lets out a sound that's between a laugh and a groan. "No, Frank, you really don't."

"I do. I can make my own decisions. Don't treat me like I'm so fragile."

"But you are. You are fragile, and the last thing I'd ever want to do is break you."

"You won't, Jonas. I promise. So just kiss me."

Another groan, only this one sounds more like a growl.

Without another argument, he hauls me against him, his hands running over my curves and down, down, down until they slide under my butt and he lifts me. On instinct—because it's surely not based on experience—I wrap my legs around his waist.

I'm not stupid, and I've read plenty of romance novels I'm definitely *not* supposed to read. I know what I'm feeling between my legs is proof Jonas is loving the feel of his lips on mine just as much as I am.

Just like somehow, deep down, even though I didn't plan it, I knew this weekend wasn't just him coming over to work on our chemistry project.

It was more.

I knew it when I asked him. Knew it when he said yes. Knew it when his knuckles rapped against the door and when I stood on the other side almost wishing he'd leave and we wouldn't fall into this trap we so carefully placed for ourselves.

I knew it when I asked him to come in.

And I wanted it all along.

I wanted *this*.

To touch Jonas. To feel him.

To kiss him.

Suddenly we're moving, and if I'm not mistaken, he's headed straight for the living room.

I pull my mouth from his, looking around. Yep, that's exactly where he's striding off to.

"How do you know where you're going?"

"Instinct."

I eye him and he laughs.

"Okay, fine—I snooped when I went out to my car." He grins at me as we stop in front of the couch. "I was curious and you're a horrible host. You didn't even give me a tour or show me your room."

I don't know why, but my eyes widen at *your room* leaving his lips.

My *room?* Jonas in *my* room…?

The thought thrills and scares me all at once. No boy has ever been in my room. Heck, I think I can count on one hand the number of times my father has been in my room.

It's my place. My sanctuary. The one place I can go and not feel pressured by my parents or anyone else. It's all mine. Sharing it with someone else, even Jonas, intimidates me.

As if he can feel my fear, he sets me down on my feet but doesn't move away. I'm still practically plastered against him. With one hand on my hip, he cups my cheek with the other, brushing his thumb back and forth in both spots. I can't decide which gentle touch I like more.

"Hey, I was teasing. Like I said, I'm not here for anything, Frank."

I nod. "I know."

"If you want to stop this now and finish our project and send me on my way, I'm cool with that."

"Why do you keep trying to get me to make you leave?"

He grimaces. "Because I shouldn't have come here in the first place."

"I asked you to."

"Yeah." He nods. "But I knew better."

I don't tell him I knew better too.

"I'm just trying to give you an out here, Frank. Because of your pace."

"My pace?"

His grip tightens on my waist, squeezing me twice. "Yes."

My pace?

My pace is fast and frazzled. It's unskilled and desperate.

Because this weekend? It's *all* we have until college.

Sure, I'll see him at school every day, but despite us sitting next to each other, miles are separating us there, never mind the entire summer we'll be apart.

College is months away.

I can't wait months.

I've touched Jonas. Tasted him. I can't just let *this* be it until then.

I *have* to have more.

Right now.

Refusing to think about it, I move.

He follows.

We've swapped positions, and when I reach out and give him a gentle shove, he falls to the couch.

This time it's me who follows.

Placing a hand on his broad shoulder, I swing a leg over his lap and settle myself until I'm straddling him.

Jonas doesn't hesitate to touch me this time.

His hands go right for my hips again, like he can't *not* hold on to me.

"What are you doing, Frank?"

"Going at my own pace."

He stares into my eyes, looking for any sign of uncertainty.

He's not going to find it.

This is what I want.

Him. *All* of him.

When he doesn't find what he's looking for, he concedes. His fingers begin to move against me, digging into the curves of my hips. His thumb sweeps against my bare skin, and I love how rough it feels. I love more that I know it's from him working in his dad's auto shop because that's the kind of guy Jonas is—the kind to help his family out whenever he can.

His fingers slip higher under my shirt and I know he hears the way my breathing starts to pick up. It's suddenly hot in here, so darn hot, and I'm burning up.

I shrug my cardigan off without thought, and not until Jonas gasps do I understand why what I've done is such a big deal.

Grinning up at him, I say, "They're just shoulders, Jonas."

"But I've never seen them before." He reaches out, tracing a finger over the skin that's exposed.

I felt daring when I dressed for today and put on something I hardly ever wear—a spaghetti-strapped shirt.

"This feels very reminiscent of the old days when women weren't allowed to show their ankles for fear of turning a man on."

He bites his bottom lip, tipping his head back with a groan. "God, I bet your ankles are so fucking sexy."

"I like it when you do that."

"What?" He grins, his eyes dancing with a mixture of amusement and desire. "Fantasize about your ankles?"

"No." I laugh, shaking my head. "I like it when you say...*that* word."

He frowns. "You shouldn't, Frank."

"Why not?"

"Because you're good. Good girls don't cuss, and they definitely don't like boys who do."

Good girl—I hate that it's who I've become because of who my parents are, because of their influence. It's frustrating because I am not them.

I'm *me*.

And Jonas knows *me*.

Which means right now, with him, I don't have to hide. I don't have to worry about his judgments.

Dragging my hand up from his shoulder, my fingers crash through his thick hair, pulling on the strands just like he pulled on mine. I've wanted to touch him for months, and now I can.

Using him as leverage, I drag myself closer to him, relishing the feel of him between my legs. There's a tiny voice inside my head screaming at me that I shouldn't find this pleasurable, but I shut it out quickly.

I *do* find this pleasurable.

Very much so, in fact.

So much that I move again.

"Christ, Frank." He slams his eyes shut, hissing at the contact, and his hands fall back to my hips, holding me tightly like he wants to pull me closer but keep me at bay all at once.

I lean into him, letting my lips hover just above his, so close I can feel our mouths brushing against one another with each heavy breath we take.

"Well, I guess I'm no good girl then, because I *definitely* like boys who cuss."

"Fuck," he mutters, and I laugh, because I don't think he did it on purpose; it's just a natural reaction for him.

"What does that make me now, Jonas?"

"Good. Still good."

"Would a good girl invite you up to her room?"

His eyes snap open, and the first thing I notice is the burning fire churning in his verdant green gaze.

"Are you sure?"

I bob my head up and down. "I'm sure."

He doesn't waste another second. Holding on to me tightly, he pushes us off the couch and races up the stairs.

"Which room?"

"Why are you running? I didn't say we're having sex."

His eyes widen.

"Well, at least not right now."

His steps falter and we nearly go tumbling to the floor. He catches himself on the wall, glaring down at me. With a grin, I shimmy down his body, dropping back onto my feet but still holding on to his big shoulders.

He still has one hand on the wall, the other on my waist—which seems to be a favorite spot of his—and his hard eyes are burning into me. "You absolutely can*not* just say things like that, Frank."

"Which part? That we're having sex? Or that we're not having it right now?"

"Fucking hell." He slaps his palm against the wall. "You're killing me here."

"You'll live." I pat his cheek. "I'm only teasing you. We're not having sex...right now." I wink, and he groans. "Come on, it's at the end."

I lead him down the hall with false bravado in each step.

I'm nervous to have a boy in my room, especially when that boy is him.

And especially when he makes me feel the way I do.

Seen.

We step into my sacred place, and I hold my breath as Jonas lets his eyes wander around the small, mostly white room.

I watch as he takes in the twin-sized bed covered in a neat, light pink bedding set. There's a white dresser that matches my bed and a bookshelf that's in desperate need of rearranging, the books spilling over the shelf's capacity.

But he quickly skips over all of that.

His look lingers on the art adorning the walls. I know he's aware they're my drawings. I've doodled in our notebook enough for him to know my style. One time, without thinking, I drew him. Though we have a rule about not ripping pages out, that one mysteriously went missing.

He steps farther into the room, walking toward the one wall where my drawings hang. Some are finished, and some are works in progress because something is missing I just can't put my finger on. He studies each one with careful eyes.

Slowly, he shifts his stare to me, almost like he doesn't want to look away from the pictures. When his eyes find mine, the adoration that's shining so clearly makes my stomach do flips.

"It's a real damn shame you're not doing anything with your art, Frank. Your talent astounds me."

"I'm not that great." I look to my pieces and point toward one of the things that bothers me the most about my hobby. "My shading needs work. My eyes could use more practice too. And my—"

The sudden feeling of Jonas' fingers on my face cuts my words off.

He pulls my attention to him.

"Just take the compliment, Frank."

I nod, because there's something about the way he says it that I can't argue with. "Thank you."

"I love your art. I love the way you put a little bit of yourself into each piece you create."

"You don't know that. You haven't seen a lot of my art."

"I've seen enough to know. Besides, you're *you*—of course you leave a part of yourself inside each drawing. I'm just sorry your parents don't acknowledge this side of you." His thumb tracks over my chin and his eyes fall to my parted lips. "It's probably one of my favorites."

My breath picks up, and I briefly wonder if I'll always feel like the air is being ripped from my lungs when he's around.

"Another."

He brings his eyes back to mine, and his brows scrunch together in question.

"Tell me another favorite thing."

"Your shoulders."

"They're just shoulders." I roll my eyes at him.

He grins, stepping closer. "Your ankles."

"You've never even seen my ankles," I argue as he slides his arm around my waist and drags me into him.

"I don't need to. I bet they're *super* hot."

"You are s-so—"

My words falter when he grazes my neck with his nose, running it up the length, breathing me in.

"So what?"

"A-Annoying," I finish, clutching his shoulders as my knees begin to shake.

"Huh. You're not *acting* like I'm annoying."

"You are. Trust me."

"Duly noted. Oranges."

"Apples."

"What?"

"Oh, I thought we were just naming random fruits." I smirk.

He shakes his head then places a soft kiss on my jaw. Then another just a few centimeters above the last. "You always smell like oranges. That's one of my favorite things too."

26

"I love orange juice."

"I know, Frank." Another kiss. "I see you with it every morning."

"Oh. Right."

He chuckles, and I can feel it right down to my toes. "Your shyness."

"Seriously?"

"Yeah, it's cute. Just like your hair." He tugs on the ends of the wild strands, something he keeps doing—something I'm starting to love, which is weird because I hate my crazy hair. "Just like your glasses too."

"I want contacts *so* bad."

He kisses me again. And again. His lips are getting dangerously close to my lips now. "Just like your eyes. They're cute too. I've never seen brown eyes so full of—"

"Shit?" I say. "Because they're the color of poop."

He laughs again. "You want to know my favorite thing about you, Frank?"

I nod in response, because there's no way I could talk in this moment even if I tried. Not when his lips are so, so close to mine.

"Your mouth."

And he proves it to me.

I was right.

My world did shift.

A boy stayed the night.

A boy stayed the night at my house. In my *bed*.

Not just any boy.

Jonas.

I'm falling for him.

I know it sounds silly and probably a little stupid, but I can't help it. He makes me feel so...*me*.

It's not just his kisses—which are incredible, and I'm practically an expert in them now because all we did last night was kiss. Over and over again.

No, it's more than that.

It's the way he makes me laugh. The way he looks *at* me, not through me. The way he talks to me, not at me.

It's everything. *He's* everything.

"What kind of sprinkles do you want?" Jonas shouts from the bottom of the stairs. He's been in the kitchen for the last five minutes making us sundaes.

Junk food is a big no-no in our house, so every time my parents go out of town, I feast on whatever I want.

With Jonas coming over this weekend, I *might* have gone a little overboard with it. I loaded up on chips, cookies, crackers...and enough supplies to make roughly six sundaes.

"Yes!" I reply from my perch on my bed, sketchpad in hand, pencil flying over the page as I work on my latest creation.

He laughs. "Roger that." Another minute passes then I hear, "Incoming!"

He bounds up the stairs and down the hall, appearing in my doorway with two massive bowls of ice cream. Both are piled high with the last of our supply of candies, sprinkles, and crumbled-up cookies.

I have no idea why we're eating this—again—but we have to.

Jonas leaves tonight. My parents are coming home bright and early in the morning.

Technically he could stay, and we'd just wake up super early, but we decided it's best not to risk it.

28

I'm trying not to think about it, trying hard just to focus on the now and not anything else.

"Stop thinking about it or you're not getting your ice cream." He stands above me, bowl in hand, brows lifted high. "And you'd really be bummed because this is my best fucking sundae so far."

My cheeks color at the foul language, and he doesn't miss it.

Ever since I told him I like it when he says it, he keeps using it.

I think it's just so I'll crawl into his lap and kiss him again. Joke's on him, because I'd do it anyway just to feel him against me again.

I set my sketchpad down and hold my hands out. "I'm not thinking about it. Give me the goods."

"Come on," he says, nodding toward the floor. "Let's eat over here, under the stars."

"They're not real stars, Jonas." I roll my eyes but scoot off the bed anyway, following him.

During one of our many make-out sessions last night, Jonas realized I have some of those glow-in-the-dark stars stuck to my ceiling and quickly became entranced by them. Since then he's been making us eat all our meals under them.

"I know, but they're as close to a romantic meal under the stars as we're gonna get until college. Now sit."

I do. He hands me my bowl of ice cream as he takes a seat with his own.

"I can't wait until college."

"Me either." He shoves a couple huge bites in. "The faster we get through college, the faster I can get to the NFL."

"Oh, planning for the big leagues, huh?"

"Every damn day, baby."

Skip-skip goes my heart at the endearment.

"But don't think I'm wanting those four years to just pass me by. I'm going to be spending every free moment I have between classes and practices with you."

My movements halt when he discusses a future between us so freely. We've talked a lot about going to school together in our notebook. We didn't plan it—because I'd much rather be going elsewhere for college—but as soon as we found out we'd be heading off to the same school come fall, it was all we could talk about.

The possibilities.

Shoveling another bite into my mouth, I try not to think about it and what his words imply, because what if I'm just twisting his words? What if Jonas doesn't want to actually *date* me? Dating is a whole lot different than kissing.

"Don't think I didn't see that little pause. What'd I say?"

I peek over at him. "N-Nothing."

Jonas laughs at the ice cream that begins to dribble down my chin. He reaches over, using his thumb to wipe away the mess.

That part doesn't surprise me. He's been touching me without hesitation all weekend.

What shocks me is when he sticks his thumb in his mouth, licking the sweet sticky goodness clean like it's no big deal.

I gulp at the action, wishing I were his thumb right now.

"First, you're a mess. Second, it's not nothing. Is it because I said I want to spend time with you?"

I nod.

"And that's…a surprise to you?"

"Yes," I tell him honestly. "I know we've talked about going away to college together, but I don't know exactly what that means."

Jonas sighs and sets his half-eaten bowl of ice cream to the side.

I do the same with mine when he gestures for me to lie down.

We both do, side by side, staring up at the stars. Our hands are resting next to each other, our pinkies rubbing together.

We lie there for several quiet minutes…so long I start to count the stars on the ceiling to distract myself from the quiet.

"What do you want it to mean?" Jonas finally says.

I don't answer right away. Not because I don't know, but because I'm scared he won't like the answer.

"Because for me, Frank, it means *us*. And not just hanging out."

Even *I* hear my sharp inhalation.

He rolls to face me, and I mirror his position.

He watches me, waiting for an answer.

"Would…would that be okay?"

I've seen Jonas nearly every day for the last four years, which means I've seen many versions of him.

Tired Jonas who stayed up too late partying the night before.

Exhausted Jonas who spent a crazy number of hours on the football field.

Sad Jonas when his grandma passed two Novembers ago.

Happy Jonas who just won yet another championship.

I've even encountered Flirty Jonas a time or two.

But never have I ever seen Jonas like he is now.

Nervous.

I like that he's nervous. It means he's serious about what he just said, what he's asking.

Jonas wants more than this too.

"Yes."

He breathes a sigh of relief, rolling to his back, clutching his chest. "Fuck, Frank. Don't tease me like that."

I swat at him. "Shush."

He rolls back my way with a grin. "I'm kidding. I knew you'd say yes."

"Oh, you did?"

"Definitely."

"And how'd you know that?"

31

"Because I can feel it in your kisses."

"Can you?"

He nods. "Yep. You want me."

I do. "You're dreaming."

"Only of you, baby."

I laugh. "How cliché."

He moves quickly and before I know it, I'm trapped under him. This position of ours has become familiar over the last twenty-something hours, and every time I find myself under his weight, those same butterflies start up in my stomach again.

"Cliché, but true."

"I can't believe I let you kiss me," I tease.

He stares at me for just a moment, and something in his eyes makes my breath catch. He looks like he wants to say something but thinks better of it.

Instead, he lowers his lips to mine and says, "Yes you can."

Then he's kissing me like he's trying to prove his point.

It's made when I slide my hands into his hair, holding him to me.

It's proven yet again when a soft moan escapes me the second his fingertips crawl across my skin.

It's upheld when he peels my shirt off, and then his own. When he lays me back down wearing nothing but nerves and yearning.

And when I never tell him to stop, it's verified that not only do my kisses tell him I want a future with him, they say something else.

I've completely fallen for Jonas Schwartz.

Slice Three

JONAS

NOW

"If I have to listen to you say 'go deeper' one more time, I will murder you."

"Well, then go deeper!"

"I can't just *go deeper*. That's not how it works."

"That is *exactly* how it works."

My hand is raised, prepared to knock as I stand at the customer's door, unabashedly listening to the very loud conversation the couple is having, brows raised with so many questions running through my mind.

The first one being, *Did I* really *have to make a spectacle and almost blow my chance in the NFL so I can deliver pizzas for a living?*

Answer: no. No, I did not.

But here I am. Standing at the door, pie in my hand, listening to some chick and her boyfriend go on about how he needs to go deeper.

I don't know who I feel worse for in this situation, the chick or the dude.

Poor dude has a small dick, and she's not being taken care of.

*What a pre*dick*ament to be in.*

With reluctance—because I really don't want to have to see my *third* naked couple today—I rap my knuckles against the door.

There's the now all-too-familiar shuffle.

The hushed, "They're here! Grab the money!"

I brace myself for the swinging dick I'm about to encounter as I hear the knob turning.

The door is flung open and, to my surprise, the person standing in front of me is fully clothed.

And *hot.*

I will not check out the customers. I will not check out the customers.

I focus on the task at hand, pulling open the insulated pizza bag.

"Good even—"

"Holy moly." The words drop from her plump lips on a whisper, her big, brown eyes widening. "Jonas."

My brows shoot up when she addresses me by name, and I give her my full attention.

Something about her seems familiar, but I can't recall where I've seen her. Maybe a party or two? There's only one person I've ever met with hair her color, but there's no way that's who is standing before me now.

I trail my eyes down the woman's body. I know I didn't hook up with her—I'd remember a body like hers. I let my eyes linger a moment, enjoying the way her jade tank top clings to her curves and stands out against her pale skin before getting my shit together and bringing my gaze back to her face. Her mouth is still ajar, the shock of me standing at her door not yet having worn off.

Even if I don't know who she is, she definitely knows who I am.

I guess that's what happens when you have an amazing college football career, so great that you're headed for the NFL when you graduate, and then when you're high on winning a bowl game, you jump onto the railing of the bleachers and…fall straight on your ass. Or, in my case, directly on your knee in just the right way to put you out of commission, shattering and tearing not only it but all your NFL dreams, leaving you to deliver pizzas in your hometown while you work on physical therapy.

It's been a long six months.

Clearing my throat, I push my shoulders back. "Good evening. I have a large pepperoni and extra cheese on hand-tossed crust with two ranch dipping sauces." I slide the pizza out with ease and shove it her way. "That'll be $10.47."

She doesn't take the pie.

"I'm not imagining this. You are Jonas Schwartz, right?"

I sigh, slightly annoyed the ball cap I'm wearing and the beard I grew aren't enough to hide behind. "I am. Have we met before?"

"Well, I'll be damned. Nice to see ya, Schwartzy."

The guy steps into view, and I recognize him instantly. Despite having attended the same college, I haven't had a proper conversation with the guy since my freshman year when I got wasted and told him about what happened with Frankie.

I've seen him around campus a few times since, but he mostly hung out with the theater kids, which definitely wasn't the crowd I was running with.

"Well fucking well," I drawl. "Julian Schenn. How the hell are you, man?"

"Not bad, not bad. Helping my girl here put together her bookshelf. She can't seem to understand you have to put the screws all the way in and not just leave them sticking out."

Ah, so that's what go deeper meant.

The girl stares daggers at him, crossing her arms over her chest, pushing her tits up. *Stop noticing, you dick.*

"First, I am *not* your girl. Second, I was going as deep as I could."

"Sure you were. You just gotta put a little more muscle behind it, that's all."

She holds her arm up, flexing her bicep. "You see these guns? I was putting *all* the muscle into it."

He squeezes her nonexistent guns. "You're still using that two-pound weight, huh? Need a spotter next time you hit the gym?"

She socks him in the gut, and I can't help but laugh as he grunts. She might not have muscles, but she can apparently pack a punch.

"I yield," he wheezes. "Schwartz, you remember Callahan, right?"

Callahan? There's only one Callahan I've ever known, and there is no way this chick standing in front of me is her.

It's impossible…right?

But my eyes see the undeniable truth.

Right there, just below her left eye, is the scar I remember so fondly.

It *is* her.

"Frank."

Her cheeks redden at the nickname I gave her in high school, and my palms begin to sweat in response to the reality of being face to face with her.

For four long years, I looked for her, scouring social media. Checking every face at every party, hoping she'd appear. We were set to attend the same college, but not once did we run into each other.

Turns out, I wasn't looking for the girl I knew at all.

In high school, she was all frizz with big, bulky glasses covering her pale face. She always reminded me of Anne Hathaway from that damn movie my sister Thea used to make me watch over and over.

I guess Frankie had her own *The Princess Diaries* moment, because right now she looks a hell of a lot more like Mia Thermopolis *after* the makeover.

I'll never admit this out loud, but even though Mia was hot as fuck after that transformation, I always kind of preferred her with the frizz.

Which is exactly why I could barely stand having Frankie as my lab partner our senior year.

It wasn't that I didn't like being around her. It was the exact opposite.

Every morning she'd walk in smelling like oranges, probably from that boxed orange juice she'd toss into the trash when she stepped through the door. She'd shuffle her way to our table, slide onto her stool next to me—the one I'd drag just a few centimeters closer each day—then reach into her bag for a piece of orange-flavored gum, offering me one too. It didn't matter that I turned down her every offer; she was still the politest lab partner ever, and she'd still try.

Without fail, this was our routine.

I made sure to take my vitamin C every fucking day so I wouldn't get sick and miss a second of the seventy-five minutes I had with her. It was the first time in my high school career I didn't have any absences.

It's not like I showed up for the conversation. Hell, we probably only spoke a handful of sentences to one another out loud the entire time we were in school together.

But that didn't mean we didn't talk.

Every day I had to sit next to her while she sat in silence, chewing on that damn bottom lip of hers and hiding behind the ball of frizz she called hair.

It was annoying…yet I couldn't stop stealing glances at her.

I loved the way she'd let her glasses fall to the end of her nose before pushing the center piece until they were tucked back into place. I adored the way she'd line up her notebook and pencils in the same order, ensuring everything was straightened out before she flipped open her notebook, always adding the date in the top right corner in the most precise handwriting I'd ever seen. And when her mind would wander, she'd chew on the ends of her pencils until they were all marked up and unusable.

I'd never wanted to be an inanimate object so badly in my life.

By that first Friday, the silence and miles spanning between us were killing me.

I *needed* to talk to her.

On a whim, I scribbled a frivolous note and slid the paper her way.

I'm 75% sure Ms. Day just farted.

I watched as the corner of her lips ticked up and she reached for the third pencil in her lineup, chewing on the end of it for a moment or two before finally bringing the utensil to paper.

Only 75%?

Just two words, and I knew I had her.

We managed to fill five notebooks during those 180 days. She'd take it home one evening, and I would the next. Sometimes our entries were lengthy, packed with our deepest, darkest confessions. Sometimes it was nothing but a doodle—well, a masterpiece in her case, and in mine, a crude drawing a kindergartener could have out-scribbled.

Nothing was off limits.

Our aspirations, fears, strongest desires, and embarrassing confessions…it was all there between the pages.

Inside those cheap notebooks, there were no rules, no social ladders, no lines.

It was just us.

We spent the entire school year like this, our stools moving ever closer together, elbows rubbing as we worked silently side by side for months.

Until we hit a snag in whatever it was we were doing.

We had an end-of-the-year project due and were required to work on it outside classroom hours.

The moment our teacher proposed this, I knew I was screwed.

Frankie Callahan was not to be touched…especially not by me.

Everyone in school knew it. She was the one person you didn't mess with.

Yet, there I was, watching her every day like a fucking creep, eager to see if she'd show up smelling like oranges.

There I was…wanting her.

Somehow, during the month we had to work on the project, we managed to keep our interactions limited to the library and courtyard. I think we both knew what being alone would mean.

At least I thought we were on the same page.

Frankie had other plans.

"Uh, J-Jonas?"

It's the first time she's said my name out loud, and a warmth like no other spreads through me.

I blink up at her, surprised to find her even speaking to me.

She rushes to apologize. "S-Sorry, I didn't mean to startle you."

"You didn't."

"Oh." She clears her throat. "I-I just… W-We…" She pauses, shaking her head at herself for all the stuttering. "I believe we should move the rest of our project elsewhere. It's going to require a lot of cutting and gluing, and I don't think we should be doing that around all these"—she waves a hand toward the stacks—"precious beauties."

My lips quirk up at her choice of words. "Precious beauties, huh?"

Her cheeks fill with color, and I realize in that moment her blushing is one of my favorite sights. "What can I say? I'm a bit of a book lover."

"You?" I fake gasp. "Say it ain't so, Frank."

"It's Frankie," she says.

I study her. "Nah, you look like more of a Frank to me."

She doesn't say anything else but seems pleased by me giving her a nickname, and I want to slap myself for flirting because anything happening between us just isn't possible.

I'm Jonas Schwartz, captain of the football team. I score off the field just as much as I do on it. I'm known for letting things get a bit too wild, and the only time I've ever shown any restraint is in first period chemistry when I have to sit next to her every morning.

She's Frankie Callahan…the pastor and the principal's daughter.

Enough said.

"What were you getting at, Callahan?" I ask.

"O-Oh. I, uh, well, my parents are out of town this weekend."

"They leave you home alone?"

"I'm responsible," she says haughtily, and it's the first time I've heard her have even a hint of attitude.

She's…fiery.

I kind of like Fiery Frank.

"So, do, uh, do you want to come over this weekend?"

My heart rate picks up at the thought of being alone with Frank. There are so many things that could happen. So many things I want to happen. So many things that shouldn't happen.

If I go over there, she'll try to kiss me. And I'll let her.

The last thing she needs is to be tainted by my use-'em-and-lose-'em reputation. If someone were to find out we were hanging out outside of school hours…well, let's just say that wouldn't work out well for either of us.

We'd be alone though…

"You, uh, you could come in the back. Stay the night. It would be just us."

Just us.

No one would ever have to know. They'd never even know I was there. We could spend the entire weekend together, do whatever we wanted, live in our own little world.

It's a bad idea. The worst idea she's ever had. The foulest idea in the history of ideas.

But, if there is anything people know about me, it's that I love a good bad idea.

"Jonas?"

Two syllables. A bat of her lashes.

That's all it takes.

"Yes."

"It's Frankie," she spits at me.

Clearly, she's still pissed about what happened between us.

Just as I had predicted, Frankie tried to kiss me.

And just as I'd promised, I let her.

She climbed into my lap and we spent way too long on her couch, kissing and touching each other. Exploring.

We fell asleep, wrapped together in her twin bed.

We cooked breakfast on Sunday, unable to keep our hands to ourselves at every turn. It didn't matter that our lips were sore and swollen. We knew our time together was limited, and we didn't want to waste a second.

Our last afternoon together, we lay on her bedroom floor, counting the silly glow-in-the-dark stars she had stuck on the ceiling.

I don't know how it happened, but eventually we were nothing but a mess of limbs.

Her shirt came off. Mine followed. And then she was trusting me with something special as I slid into her warmth.

"I'm sorry. I know it hurts."

"Then make it feel better."

I did.

And then we heard it—tires turning onto the pavement.

We were supposed to have a few more hours.

Her parents were home early.

I threw my clothes on as fast as I possibly could and beat feet out the back door, thankfully having been smart enough to park three blocks over so nobody would see my car in the drive.

That was the first and only time Frankie and I slept together—I made sure of it.

The next morning, she passed me our notebook.

I'm sorry. Can we talk later? Alone somewhere?

Her perfect handwriting came into view, and I wanted to rip the book from her hands and toss it into the trash.

But I didn't.

Instead, I wrote the one word I should I have said to her before.

No.

Her sharp inhale ripped a hole through my chest. Heads turned our way as her bottom lip began to quiver and tears sprang to her eyes.

I said nothing, instead turning my attention to the front of the room, staring daggers at anyone who dared look my way.

Frankie fled.

I stayed.

It was the last time we ever spoke.

Until now.

I let my eyes wander over her body, hands aching to reach out and touch her once more. To see if her body still fits mine so perfectly. See if her tits hold the same weight they once did. If I can still fit an ass cheek in each palm. If her lips still taste like oranges.

If I can still make her gasp my name with just a flick of my fingers.

She shifts under my perusal, and I have a feeling she's thinking about the same thing I am.

"What are you doing here, Jonas?"

I don't miss the extra layer of ice she puts on her words.

She's pissed at me, and rightfully so.

I try not to laugh at her ridiculous question because it's painfully, embarrassingly obvious what I'm doing here.

"Delivering your pizza."

"No, Jonas, I mean *here*. You're not supposed to be *here*. You should be..." She huffs and gestures wildly. "Well, not here."

"You call Slice. I deliver." I lift the box. "That's how this pizza thing works."

She doesn't acknowledge my snarky response. "You should be gone."

I gnash my molars together, annoyed by the reminder. It's not the first time I've had an encounter like this, a customer informing me where I'm *supposed* to be.

I know where I'm supposed to be, and it sure as shit ain't here slinging pizzas.

But that's what happens when you shoot your career in the foot, drown your sorrows in booze, and slack on your physical therapy for two months, leaving you behind where you wanted to be.

"Yeah, well, I'm not," I say flatly.

Her hard eyes soften, and a peep of the Frankie I used to know shines through. "What happened?"

"I, um..." I shuffle the pizza onto my other hand, feeling uncomfortable as she stares at me with questioning eyes. "Well, I—"

"Damn, Frankie, quit giving the guy the third degree. He's had a rough year."

She blinks up at Julian, almost like she forgot he was here.

I did too.

"You would know that if you hadn't ditched me and run off to that fancy art school of yours for the last four years."

Art school? Is there where she's been? At my college's sister campus?

43

She drops her head, trying to hide behind her hair again just like she used to. "Stop whining."

"So you admit it then? That you ditched me?"

"I'm about to ditch your dead body somewhere," she mutters, reaching into her back pocket then shoving a wad of cash in my face. "Here. Keep the change."

A resounding *thud* echoes through the otherwise quiet apartment complex. The door is slammed so hard, I swear I hear something rattle against the wall.

"Frankie!" Schenn shouts at her, and she responds with something unintelligible.

They speak in hushed tones, and I know I shouldn't stand here and listen, but I can't move.

I found her. After years of searching and wondering and regret, I found her.

And she's pissed as hell.

Now if only she'd let me explain that I *had* to tell her no all those years ago.

I didn't have a choice.

Her parents made sure of that.

Slice Four

FRANKIE

"What the hell, Callahan? You can't just slam the door in his face like that."

"Well, I did."

I try to shoulder past my best friend, but he doesn't let me get very far, blocking my way with his giant frame. "Dammit, Julian. My pizza is getting cold."

"*Our* pizza."

I glare up at him. "*My* pizza. I didn't promise you food."

"Only because you're a bad host. Come on, Frankie—you're being rude, and it's way out of character for you."

"Rude? *Rude?*" My heart tries to burst from my chest as my temper rises. "*I'm* the one being rude? Are you kidding me right now, Jules? You know what he did to me!"

"Last I checked, *you* did it right back to him."

"Good gravy, I'm not talking about sex. I'm talking about him...well, getting his rocks off and abandoning me."

"Oh." Julian nods. "That's where you were going with that. Makes more sense."

I shake my head, trying not to fly across the hall and kill him for being so dense. "I swear, if I wasn't holding this pizza..."

He ignores my thinly veiled threat and finally moves out of my way...toward the door.

"What are you doing!" I shriek, shoving my small frame in front of him, as if puny me is going to stop the ex-linebacker.

"I'm gonna go talk to him."

"You're what? No, Julian!" I shove at him with one hand, pushing the pie under his nose. "I'll share my pizza. I promise. Just don't go talk to him."

He grabs at my shoulders, holding me back at arm's length. "Hush. I'll be right back."

He swoops by and is through the door faster than I can jump on his back with this pizza in my hand.

"Julian!" I hiss after him, and I swear I hear him laugh at me.

"Hey, man, wait up!" he says to Jonas.

I, Frankie Callahan, do something naughty, something I *know* I shouldn't be doing—plaster myself to the door and eavesdrop.

"Frank doesn't like me very much, huh?"

Julian chuckles. "You could say that."

I glower at him through the door.

Don't bother pretending to be shocked, Jonas. You're a terrible actor.

Well, that's not true.

He spent *months* acting like he liked me, and I fell for every one of his charms.

"Not like I don't deserve her wrath, but it's..."

Their voices trail off, and I push my eye up to the peephole, annoyed to see them walking away.

Julian looks back and winks.

The jerk knows I'm spying on them.

I fall back against the door, feeling drained like I haven't in years.

The last person I expected to see when I opened the door was Jonas Schwartz, the boy I fell in love with and gave my virginity to.

The same boy who got what he wanted then never spoke to me again.

A small part of me owes a lot of thanks to Jonas for what transpired between us after our weekend together—he gave me the courage to chase my dream of going to art school.

Sure, a lot of it had to do with the fact that I couldn't possibly spend another four years attending the same school as him. Even though I lost my virginity to a liar, a master manipulator, a complete and utter jerk…I was the winner.

But he still hurt me. Crushed me. *Changed* me.

I hate him.

And yet…I miss him.

I miss his laugh. His smile. Those stupid, crude superhero doodles he'd draw. I miss the dimple in his chin and the way he'd always wipe his hands on his pants when he was nervous.

I miss his touch…his roughened, calloused hands, worn from years of playing football and working at his dad's auto shop during the off-season.

I miss knowing him like nobody else did.

A lot of people thought Jonas had it all because he was the star of the football team, but they didn't know him like I did.

He worked hard for what he had, put his all into the game, into practice, into his dad's shop. He never took any of it for granted either.

But missing him doesn't compare to how angry I am with him.

It turns out I'm not one to forgive easily.

The knob rattles as Julian tries to barge his way back into my apartment.

I scuttle away from the door and throw myself onto the couch, flinging open the pizza box and shoveling a slice into my mouth.

"Oh, hey," I say around a mouthful of food as Julian pushes the door shut behind his large frame.

If you saw the two of us walking down the street, you'd probably laugh at the image before you.

I'm on the shorter side of life, standing at just five foot three and three-quarters—at least according to my gynecologist, who stole a quarter of an inch from me at my last exam. Julian is easily six four and built like he benches refrigerators every morning.

We're our own circus when we're out and about together.

"Don't 'oh hey' me. I know you were eavesdropping."

"Who? Me?" I bat my lashes. "I would never."

"Bull." He lounges back onto my couch, easily taking up the rest of the sofa, leaving me tucked away in my little corner. "Give me that pizza."

"Heck no! This is *my* dinner. If I hand it over to you, you'll eat the whole damn thing."

"Calling me fat?"

"I'm calling you *big-boned*."

"I'll give you a big bone." He juts his hips off the couch. "Come to Papa Julian."

I roll my eyes. "In your dreams."

"We call those nightmares, sweetie."

That's the thing about Julian and me: we have *zero* attraction to one another. It's not that he's not into girls—because he's into both girls *and* boys—it's just that he's not into me, and I am perfectly okay with that.

We'd gone to school together for years but never really talked to one another until our senior year when we were both cast in a play.

When Julian Schenn, star linebacker of the Dogwood Dodgers, walked into the community theater for the first time, my jaw hit the floor. It was the last place I expected him to show up. He was all rough-and-tough jock. Theater wasn't his idea of fun.

Or at least that's what I thought.

Turns out Julian was a closet theater geek...and he was closeted about other things too. That year, working late nights prepping for the spring production, he came out to me as bisexual and confessed he didn't want to play football in college—something his parents wanted him to do desperately. Instead, he wanted to pursue the arts and was testing out every medium he could get his hands on.

We bonded over the fact that our parents were pushing us to be these people we weren't and have been inseparable since.

Well, minus the four years of college I left for.

"So...Jonas Schwartz, huh." He says it so casually, like he's *not* trying to rile me up, even though he definitely is. I eye him, eating my pizza and ignoring his wasted efforts. "Good to know he's still hot as fuck. I mean, can we *please* talk about that beard? Are we still sure he's straight? Because there are *a lot* of places I'd like to feel that thing."

There are a lot of places I'd like to feel it too.

Julian's right though—Jonas *does* look extra good with a beard.

Then again, he's always looked good.

I've technically known Jonas since I first moved here in ninth grade. My mom got a new job and my dad was ready to tackle leading a church. So, we packed up our entire lives and headed out east.

Moving is hard on a kid no matter what, but picking up one's whole life and ripping her from the only place she's known since she was born when she's a teenager...well, it's hell.

Add in the fact that I wasn't just going to be known for being the pastor's daughter but also the principal's daughter?

Yeah, count me out for any social event ever.

I withdrew.

I didn't want to talk to anyone. I became shy. A book nerd. A complete loner.

I was okay with that for the most part. A lot of it was my own doing.

That didn't mean I wasn't ever lonely.

Talk about the shock of the century when not one person in my new school took the time to acknowledge me until the first Friday of my freshman year, as least not to my face.

An entire week.

Not a single soul.

Until him.

Until Jonas.

"You're new here, right?"

I turned to my left, locking eyes with the prettiest shade of green I'd ever seen.

His jaw was square, nose sharp, and he smelled faintly of grease or oil or something along those lines.

Looking at him was intoxicating, and I was ready to get drunk.

"I-I-I am."

"I'm Jonas. It's nice to meet you."

I didn't say anything back. I couldn't. I was paralyzed by him.

"Say, do you have a pencil I could borrow? I seemed to have forgotten mine."

"S-Sure."

And that was our first encounter.

We didn't become instant best friends or anything like that, but I did feel something instantly.

Over the years, we shared more classes, but I was never lucky enough to sit next to him again until senior year. We didn't run in the same circle—okay, fine, I didn't have a circle—but our paths crossed in other ways. Overlapping gym classes. The fact that I was in band

and got to play at all his football games.

The fact that he was Jonas Schwartz and he was all over the school all the time.

Sometimes, he'd nod at me in the hall or give me a small smile, and though I knew it had nothing to do with *me* and everything to do with Jonas being friendly to everyone, it was always enough to make me giddy for weeks.

There's no denying I had a mad crush on Jonas from the first day I met him. It was a no-brainer to me that when he finally saw me for me and liked me back, I gave him my all.

Except he turned out to not be the guy I thought he was and ripped my heart out.

"My lost virginity says he is," I snark at my best friend. "Besides, you went to college with him—I'm sure you saw all the girls he was with."

"Actually, come to think of it, I can't recall a single time I saw him *with* a girl." Julian runs a hand through his hair, playing with the dark blond locks, pulling and twisting them. "Sure, there were always chicks around, but I surprisingly didn't hear many rumors about him and his extracurriculars, not like we did in high school. He kept things lowkey."

I hate the way my blood starts pumping a little faster at this new information.

I truly thought once Jonas hit college, he'd be sowing his wild oats up and down the dorms. It was one of the reasons why, at the last minute, I accepted the offer I received from the art school I'd secretly applied to. I couldn't bear the thought of having to see him with all those different girls.

It was the push I needed. I put my foot down with my parents and went to school for what I wanted to—art.

Even though I was still attending a college close by, they didn't take the news well. They didn't think an art degree would benefit me financially long-term and wanted me to pursue teaching like my mother or a business degree where the options were endless.

It took six months before my mother spoke to me again, and three and a half years for my father to accept it...which he only did because of the cancer spreading through his lungs.

Losing Jonas and any relationship I had with my father made for a tough few years.

"Basically, what I'm saying is, there is still hope he now bats for my team," Julian explains, pulling me from my mind.

"Technically"—I hold up a finger—"he does bat for your team since you bat for both."

He grabs his junk. "This team, sweetie."

"Ick." I shudder. "Pass on *that* junk."

"Oh, I see how it is. *My* junk isn't good enough for you, but you'll take Schwartz's junk. Noted." He grins smugly, and I want to slap it off his face. "It's the beard, isn't it? Because I'll grow one, baby." He winks. "I bet I'd look hot as fuck too."

I groan. "Why are you still here? The shelf is assembled. Your services are no longer needed."

"You're telling me you've been using me?" He holds a hand to his chest. "And here I thought you invited me over because you like my company."

"If I liked your company, I'd have gotten pizza for two."

"Rude."

"But true."

I grab another slice and try to ignore the holes he's staring into the side of my head, but it's difficult. He's so big and takes up so much room; he's hard to ignore.

"What?" I finally ask. "Out with it already. I know you have something to say, so just say it."

"How do you know I have something to say?"

"Because you *always* have something to say."

"Fair." He laughs. "What are you gonna do about Jonas being back?"

"What do you mean back? You two only went to college an hour away. *I'm* the one who's back."

He groans, clearly annoyed by me playing dumb. "You know what I mean, Frankenstein." He jostles me with his giant foot. "Now that you're both back in the same town for the first time in four years, what are you gonna do?"

"What I always do: pretend he doesn't exist."

"Do you really think that's the best play? I saw the way he looked at you just now, and he didn't exactly look upset to see you. He was too busy appreciating the new you."

The new me—I'm still not used to her.

After landing my dream job, I got my wild hair straightened and got contacts. It's amazing what a haircut and taking your glasses off can do for you.

I must admit, I hate how right he is. Jonas *didn't* look upset to see me, something that elates me and makes me sad all at once.

Why couldn't he see me in high school? Why couldn't he have looked at me like that back then? So...excited?

Just because he's doing it now doesn't change anything.

I'm still mad. I'm still not over what happened.

"Yes. Ignoring Jonas and pretending he doesn't exist is most definitely the best play."

"You trying to convince me of that or yourself?"

"If I wasn't so in love with this pizza, I'd throw it at you."

"I doubt that. Besides, I'm leaving—need to get started on that project for Barry."

Ah, good old Barry, chief executive of Allen Illustrations where

Julian and I both work. I'm in the design department and he's with the writers. The medium Julian settled on is the written word, and he's damn good at it.

He pushes himself off the couch, standing over me, hands on his hips.

I stare up at him, a slice of my pie hanging from my mouth. "Can I help you?"

With the reflexes of a cat, he snatches two slices from the box in my lap and holds them up in victory.

"Ha! Sucker!"

"What the heck! You pizza thief! That's a felony!"

"Oh really?" He raises a brow at me. "Stealing pizza is a felony? How so?"

"Well, it's not technically, but it should be because pizza is the most priceless thing on our planet. Besides, how are you going to drive and eat two slices of pizza at the same time? You don't have enough hands."

"Like this." Julian slaps the two slices together, cheese side in, and takes a huge bite out of his creation. "See?"

"That's genius, but I still hate you for stealing my pizza. Be gone, you thief!"

Rolling his eyes, he leans down and smacks a loud kiss to my cheek. "I'll see you later, *Frank*."

My eyes narrow to slits.

"What?" he questions, backing away toward the door. "I can't call you that, but Jonas can?"

Yes. "No."

"Uh-huh. Sure." Another wink. "I'll see you tomorrow?"

"It's Monday, so I guess so."

"Don't forget the donuts. It's your turn."

"Ugh." I groan. "That means I'll have to get up early."

"It's for donuts—it's worth it."

"For you." I shake the pizza at him. "I had breakfast plans already."

"I'm sorry, but you were going to have leftovers and you *still* weren't going to offer me any pizza?"

"Nope."

"I don't know if I should be mad and say you're the worst best friend ever, or if I should let you see my boner right now."

"Julian!" I grab whatever's sitting next to me on the table and chuck it his way.

He blocks the coaster effortlessly with his meaty paw that could double as a glove. "Ha! Missed."

"Get out!"

"I'm going, I'm going."

He pulls open the front door, takes one step out, and pauses again, looking back at me with sad eyes.

I sigh. "What now?"

"You're gonna be mad."

His eyes aren't sad; they're guilty.

"Julian...what did you do." It doesn't come out a question, more of a threat.

He shoots me a sweet smile.

"Well," he drawls out, "I kind of made a date for us."

I feel the color drain from my face, shaking my head, eyes wide. "You didn't. Please tell me you didn't."

"I did. We're having drinks with Jonas tomorrow night."

"But...why? Why would you do that to me?"

He lifts a shoulder. "Because, Frankie, it's time you got some fuckin' answers. If you're too chickenshit to question Jonas, I will. I respected your boundaries when you were away for school, but after seeing the way you looked at him and reacted to him tonight, it's clear there's still something eating at you. Besides, you need a night out. You're dealing with a lot with your dad. Let's go out and let loose."

He's got me there. I am struggling with my father.

I'm irritated with him for cutting ties when I chose my version of happiness and not his. He missed out on my entire college career because of his stubbornness. My art was displayed in two prominent galleries, and the intractable man refused to attend either events. I had my art printed in a national magazine and didn't even get a phone call or *Good job* text.

He abandoned me because I wasn't fitting into his mold.

So, yeah, I'm angry.

But I'm also scared because the cancer isn't getting any better. It's spreading, and he might not be around much longer to be angry at.

I could use a drink or two to keep the anger at bay—anger at both my father *and* Jonas.

"I don't want answers. I just want to move on."

He gives me a look. He knows better than anyone that any attempts I've made at moving on have been futile.

No matter how angry I am, I can't seem to stay away.

It always comes back to Jonas, and I'm starting to think it always will.

He shrugs again. "Just think about it. I'll see you tomorrow. And don't forget the—"

"Donuts." I roll my eyes. "Yeah, I heard you."

"Night, Frankenstein."

"Night, Igor."

Slice Five

JONAS

"Thanks for staying late and helping. We appreciate it, son." Simon Daniels, my boss and the owner of Slice, claps me on the back. "I'm sure you have much better things to do than help out around here."

"It's no problem, Mr. Daniels. It's kind of nice being back at the old hang."

"We're glad you're here—not just because of the added hands, but because we've been getting extras calls about sending out *the* Jonas Schwartz to deliver a pizza." He winks at me, teasing me about the fact that no less than four groups of high school girls came in today to see me. The joys of working in your hometown. "Helps drum up some business."

"Sorry about them," I mutter.

"Don't be. We're lucky to have you back. It's been too long since we've seen you around these parts."

"Well, I'm back for now." I shake my leg at him. "But as soon as I get this old knee moving right again, I'm gone."

"You better be, and I better get a shout-out when you're rich and famous. After all, I was the first to employee your sorry, broke ass." He gives me another pat. "You're free to go when you're done wiping down these booths. I'll clock ya out."

"Thanks, Mr. Daniels."

"Dammit, son. Don't make me tell you again—it's Simon."

"Thanks, Simon," I correct.

He leaves me to finish up, and I'm done within five minutes. I don't waste any time sitting around shooting the shit with the crew and race out to my car.

I don't have long to get home and shower before I have to meet Frankie and Julian at The Doorway.

Luckily, Slice isn't far from my childhood home—a big reason why I agreed to stay and help today—and I'm pulling into the driveaway in no time.

"I'm back!" I holler when I push through the front door.

"In the kitchen, son."

I round the corner, smiling at the scene in front of me.

My mom's sitting on my dad's lap at the table, and they're enjoying a glass of wine post dinner. It's a weekly tradition for them, sitting together, sipping wine from Solo cups, and chatting about their day. It's simple, but I think it's one of the secrets of their marriage.

A lot of children would think it's gross to see their parents display such affection, but those children are dumb because I am thankful every single day my parents are still together and going strong after thirty years of marriage.

"How was your day, kiddo?" my mom asks.

"Good. We were slow up until the last few hours then I couldn't catch a break. Offered to stay late and help Simon until the rush was over."

"That place is always jam-packed after all these years. He should really consider opening another one in the area," my dad says. "I bet they'd make a fortune having one on the other end of the island."

"Probably. Would help with delivery fees, too. Maybe I'll bring it up to him."

"How was therapy this morning? Your knee doing any better?"

There it is, the question I was hoping to avoid.

My knee is doing better, but it's not where I want it to be.

But, to be fair, where I want to be is on the field.

I was told three to six months to heal after surgery, but here I am at six months and I just don't have the stamina I need to be able to play an entire game.

I need to heal faster. I *have* to if I ever want to play for the NFL like I've been dreaming of for years.

I try to ignore the spark of hope in my father's eye. If he had his way, I'd stay here forever and help at his shop. It was his dream for us to join forces after college, but all that changed in high school when I made varsity my freshman year and started gaining the attention of college coaches and agents alike. Then the plan became the NFL.

It's not that my father isn't proud of me for all my sports accomplishments, but I know deep his in heart, he doesn't want me to leave him. What parent does?

I think, though, that's the worst part of all of this. I let my father down by not following his dream for me and now I've fucked everything up.

"Everything's fine," I say evasively. "I'm gonna grab a quick shower and get going."

"Where ya off to?" my dad asks, respecting my boundaries even though I know they're both dying to pepper with me questions about my recovery.

"Do you guys remember Frankie Callahan?"

"Pastor Callahan's daughter?"

I nod. "Yep."

My mom smiles fondly. "Oh yes. How could I forget the way she'd stare at you on Sundays?" She laughs. "She was so smitten with you."

"She was not," I argue.

"She was probably just surprised to see his heathen ass in church," my dad says.

"That." I point toward him. "It's that right there. I'm just a heathen."

Mom tips her cup toward me. "Can't argue with that. Are you just meeting with Frankie or other friends too?"

She tries to tamp down her eagerness, but I can see through her supposedly innocuous question.

"Julian Schenn will be there too."

My mom's excitement falters when I say this.

As much as I like Julian, I also wish it were just going to be me and Frankie. I've missed her, and I'd really like to have a little alone time with her.

But I know that's not going to be possible any time soon.

Hence our buffer, Julian—the brilliant man behind this setup.

When he followed me out into the hallway, we were all smiles and pleasantry until we were out of earshot from Frankie. Then I shoved his big ass into the wall and demanded to know what the hell was up.

After I ended things with Frankie, I was a wreck, especially because it was the last thing I wanted to do, but it was necessary at the time…at least I thought it was.

Shit was dark for a while. My life was school, drink, school, drink. Repeat, repeat, repeat. I have no idea how I graduated on time because my grades were absolute trash during my freshman year of college.

About six months into the school year, I ran into Schenn's familiar face at a party put on by the frat I was rushing.

Drunk off my ass, I told him everything that'd happened with Frankie and how I was so fucking close to throwing everything away and chasing after her…wherever she was.

Somehow, he talked me off the ledge, and I didn't do anything hasty.

But the prick didn't bother to mention he was friends with Frankie and knew exactly where it was she'd run off to.

Last night he asked if I still thought about her, and I didn't have to think about the answer.

I did.

I *do.*

At least once a week, I look for her on social media, hoping and praying she got a wild hair up her ass and made an account.

It's been that way for four years.

I regret nothing more than walking away from her, because nothing and nobody has ever made me feel the way she does.

Seen.

I suppose my answer was enough for Julian, because he offered to help me make things right and then proposed supervised drinks tonight to help get Frankie and me in the same room.

He didn't have to ask me twice.

"Okay, off to shower. You two crazy kids have a good night. Don't wait up. And, please, for the love of all things holy, wear protection. The last thing I need is another sibling. Thea is quite enough, thank you."

"Hey, you jackass! I heard that."

Thea, my older sister by three years, comes waltzing through the front door.

"She is very exhausting," my dad agrees. "Trust me, I work with her all day. *All. Day,* Jonas," he whispers dramatically.

As much as my dad used to have me help in his auto shop, it was Thea who was drawn to the trade. My father made her go to school and get all the certifications she needed before hiring her to be part of the crew and making her work her way to the top. She now manages the second location at the other end of the island and lives next to the shop.

I love my sister, and she's one of the few reasons I don't mind being home. We've always been close. She's always there to give me a good pep talk or tell me when I'm being a complete and utter moron. While Thea can come off as a little abrasive to some, she's nothing but brutally honest.

Which is probably why she's still single. There's not a guy out there brave enough to handle her ass.

"I heard that too." She eyes my father. "Old man."

"This old man signs your paychecks, so watch it, missy."

"I'm not scared of you. Mom has my back."

My mother nods. "It's true. Us ladies need to stick together."

"See, Pops? I win." Thea smiles victoriously, and I bet she'd pat herself on the back right now if she wasn't carrying a box of cookies in one hand and a coffee in the other.

"What's all that?" I ask her.

"A bribe for the parentals."

"I'm not sure you're supposed to tell them you're bribing them."

"Please." She rolls her eyes. "They knew it was a bribe the second I walked in with a full box of Daisy's cookies. We all know I'd have scarfed these things down on my own if this wasn't a bribe."

I nod. "Fair point. Well, I'll leave you to woo. I'm heading out."

"Out?" Thea's brows shoot up. "Where to?"

"Meeting some friends for drinks."

"He's meeting Frankie Callahan." My mom smiles widely, her

head clearly already brimming with ideas of romance.

"Pastor Callahan's daughter?"

"She's more than just the pastor's daughter."

"You're right—wasn't she also the principal's daughter?" Thea smarts off.

"Yes." I grit my teeth. "What's your point?"

"Don't you think she's a little out of your league?"

See? That's Thea—always straight to the point.

"Good thing she's just a friend and this is just drinks."

Thea takes a seat in the chair across from my parents, sliding the box of cookies toward them. My mother doesn't hesitate, grabbing the box and plucking a cookie out. She breaks it in half, handing some to my father. Poor guy, too, because we all know that's all he's going to get.

"Right. That's what they all say in the beginning, but drinks always turn into something more. Just wait and see."

"This coming from you, Ms. Sworn Off Men Forever? What do you know about dating?"

"Hey, just because I'm single doesn't mean I don't date." She winks. "I get around."

"Thea!" my dad hisses. "I *do not* want to hear this."

"I've had sex, Dad." She throws her hands up in the air. "Surprise!"

"You're going to be the death of me, kid." He shakes his head. "Hell, between you and all your escapades and Jonas falling off bleachers, I have my hands full."

Thea leans across the table, looking him square in the eye. "I think you meant sexcapades, Dad."

He plugs his fingers in his ears, shouting, "I'M NOT LISTENING TO THIS!"

The scene in front of me almost makes it worth me breaking my knee and being home with my family.

Almost.

"On that note, I'm out."

I give them a wave and scram before anyone else can start talking about their sex life.

I race up the stairs, checking my phone on the way and seeing I only have fifteen minutes before I'm supposed to meet Julian and Frankie, meaning I have no time to lollygag in the shower.

Probably for the best since last night I spent *way* too long doing just that.

I couldn't help it. Once the images of that red hair and those big, brown eyes hit my mind, they wouldn't leave, and I was a goner. Before I knew it, my hand was wrapped around my dick and I was standing under the stream until the water ran cold.

Once showered and changed, I spend a little more time than anticipated working my fingers through my hair for the perfect effortlessly messy look, annoyed with myself for caring so much as I press the gas a little harder to race down the streets of our small North Carolina beach town.

She's just a girl, I try to tell myself.

But I know that's not true.

Frankie isn't "just a girl". She never has been.

I remember the first time I saw her, the first day of freshman year. My schedule was a mess and I needed to get it fixed. She was standing in front of me, trying to get something or another figured out herself. I reckoned she must be new to the area, because I was certain I'd have remembered crazy red curls like that.

She spoke so softly I could barely hear her. On instinct, I stepped closer, trying to make out what she was saying.

That was the first time I smelled the oranges.

I closed my eyes, inhaling deeply, loving the fresh scent.

I was so lost in my own world that I didn't even notice her leaving and was thoroughly embarrassed when the receptionist had to call out to me twice to snap me out of it.

Imagine my surprise when she was sitting next to the only empty seat in first period history.

I spent the entire first week stealing glances at her, certain she'd peek over at any moment and catch me staring like a complete creep.

It took me until Friday to work up the courage to actually speak to her, and the only thing I could come up with was asking for a pencil.

I had an entire box of them in my backpack.

There's a tiny part of me that feels bad for asking her for a pencil every week when I had my own, but it was the only time I'd ever actually speak to her.

Unfortunately for me, we didn't have another chance to be seated together until senior year.

Then things escalated to a whole new level.

I pull into an empty spot at The Doorway and cut the engine on my old beat-up Blazer. It's a ridiculous ride held together by hopes, prayers, and a little duct tape, but I love it. She's my baby and I wouldn't trade her for the world.

Well, maybe for a Corvette, but don't tell her I said that.

I run a hand through my short beard, almost wishing I had shaved before I came, and force myself from the vehicle because I know I'll sit around overthinking this if I don't just get my ass inside.

It takes a moment for my eyes to adjust when I walk into the dimly lit favorite local hang. I glance around, looking for Julian and Frankie, but I don't see them.

They must be running late too.

"Well I'll be damned. Schwartzy's here, boys!"

My eyes are drawn toward the boisterous voice. Sitting in a booth are three guys I played football with in high school. We were tight for many years, but my patience with them grew thin over my senior year. I haven't spoken to any of them since graduation. Based on all the plans they had, I'm surprised to find them still living here.

"Hey, Drake," I say, approaching their table. "Wilson, Hill. How you guys been?"

"Not bad. Not too bad at all. Here"—Drake scoots over, patting the open spot next to him—"have a seat."

"Oh, no, I can't. I—"

"Just a few minutes? We haven't seen you since high school. Be nice to catch up a minute."

I'd rather get my own seat and wait for Julian and Frankie to show up, but I know they won't relent until I'm sitting down with them.

I glance around the joint one last time, looking for my party, feeling dejected when I don't see them, and reluctantly take a seat.

"Just a few minutes," I agree. "So, what have you guys been up to?"

"Well," Hill speaks up, "we all went off to State for a bit then decided college really wasn't our thing."

"So we came back home and started our own landscaping business," Wilson supplies.

"Now we co-manage the most profitable lawn business on the island," Drake finishes, a smile spreading across his face.

"Wow," I say. "That's amazing, guys. Congrats."

"We heard about your accident." Hill frowns sympathetically, but the sadness doesn't quite reach his eyes. "Sorry about the NFL. We were rooting for you."

Being the only one in your group of friends who's dedicated enough to put in the hours to excel at your sport of choice can lead to jealousy among those who don't agree with that line of thinking.

Drake, Hill, and Wilson have always had green eyes when it comes to my success at the sport we all love. Back in school, they'd always make comments about my game and the glory that came with how good I was at it. It might have seemed like normal locker room jabs to most, but I saw through their words.

They were jealous, plain and simple. Genuinely happy for me, but also indisputably jealous. The longer we played together and the more opportunities that came my way, the more prominent their envy became.

"Actually, I'm still playing football. Doctors say I'll make a full recovery." Their brows rise, and I bask in the jealousy that sparks in their eyes. "It's just a matter of when I'll be able to get back out there, but I'm still under contract."

"What are you doing in the meantime?" Wilson asks.

"A hell of a lot of physical therapy and delivering pizzas at Slice to keep myself sane. I was bored as shit sitting around at home, so I begged Simon Daniels for my job back."

"Oh, please. Like you'd have to beg anyone for anything. You're Jonas Schwartz—you're handed all that you want and need."

And there it is. The jab.

I knew it was coming, but that doesn't make it sting any less.

A lot of people seem to think I was given everything I have, but that's not even close to the truth.

I didn't grow up with money like the majority of kids on the island. We lived check to check every single week, but that was the price we paid so my father could pursue his dream of owning a shop of his own. My mom spent her days working in the office and running us kids back and forth to school and events.

Don't get me wrong, we weren't living off cheap noodles or anything and Thea and I always had everything we needed, but we didn't do family vacations. Our Christmas presents weren't lavish. I didn't get a brand-new car for my birthday.

I worked for everything I had, especially football, because

contrary to popular belief, the game didn't come naturally to me. In fact, when I first started playing, I hated it. I didn't like tackling—my small build wasn't built for the impact. I didn't like running—my asthma made it difficult. And I really hated all the sweating—nobody likes taking that many showers a day.

No matter how much I hated it, I had to play. My mother used to send us to every free camp she could sign us up for over the summers. She couldn't afford to lose the hours at the shop keeping us entertained at home.

It wasn't until the third summer of camp that I truly found my niche in the game.

It took three summers and two different coaches, but I finally found one who let me try out for quarterback. Even though I sucked at tackling, hated running, and didn't want to sweat…I could throw a ball like no other.

But just because I can throw, that doesn't mean I don't have to work on all those other parts.

I had to bulk up and keep up with my weightlifting routine without gaining too much mass. Running became something I did daily so I could make my lungs stronger. And the sweating…yeah, I still fucking hate that part.

All the hard work I put into improving myself and my game paid off big with a full-ride football scholarship. I brought in hundreds of fans and dozens of football scouts, benefitting not just me but the whole team.

I put in the blood, the tears, and I sure as shit put in the sweat.

I'm good at the game, but that doesn't mean I don't have to work hard at excelling.

I just wish these jackasses would see that.

The front door is pulled open and Julian waltzes in.

My breath quickens, because I know Frankie will be right behind him.

She steps into the light pouring inside, and it's as if the rays are illuminating her like a halo. Her head is thrown back in laughter at something Julian's said, and I miss seeing her smile like that.

I miss making her smile like that.

I lean around the booth, letting my eyes trail down her body.

Her red hair is wavier than it was the other day, and it reminds me of the old Frankie for a moment. She's wearing a shirt that reminds of something a pirate would wear, the sleeves big and flowy. It's hanging off her shoulders, and one of those lacy bra things that are all the rage peeks out from underneath.

My favorite part, though, are the high-waisted Daisy Dukes she's sporting, making her short legs look miles long…and her ass perfect.

She's stunning, and I'm kicking myself for missing her these last four years.

If I'd had my way, Frankie and I would have spent every free moment we had in college together. That was my plan. Once we got away from all the hoopla of small-town gossip, I wanted to officially make her mine.

I never got my chance.

The guys notice I'm distracted and move their gazes her way.

I'm instantly annoyed by the hunger I see in them.

"Damn." Drake whistles lowly. "Who's that fox?"

"That, my friends, is Frankie Callahan," Wilson tells everyone. "I ran into her last week at the Grab 'N' Grocery. She got real fuckable over the years."

I can practically hear him salivating, and I barely hold back my urge to punch him right in his face.

Drake pipes up next. "You ain't kidding. I'd bend her over in a heartbeat."

My blood boils, and I'm about two seconds from jumping across the table and choking the crap out of each of them when Frankie turns my way, the corners of her lips tilting up ever so slightly when she sees me.

My world tilts.

It's subtle, but I feel the shift.

And I don't want it righted any time soon.

But, per the usual lately, I'm shit out of luck.

It's like she catches herself, all the bad memories we share slamming into her at once, and her mouth falls into a thin line. Her body language shifts, shoulders going stiff.

Just like that, she's walled off her heart from me.

She rushes toward the door, but Julian blocks her from making a hasty exit. I try not to laugh as she glares up at him, considering their size difference and all.

I don't have to be sitting close to them to know they're talking about me. It's obvious from the glances they both keep sending my way.

Whatever Julian says seems to pacify her, and the tension sitting in her shoulders dissipates.

"I can't believe Julian Schenn gets to fuck her," Drake says as Julian and Frankie make their way past our table and pop into a booth two seats down, all eyes following her swaying hips. "Shit, man. Of all the guys out there, she picks the part-time cocksucker to take that sweet virgin pussy. I'm jealous as fuck."

"In high school I secretly hoped I could get a go at her—really stick it to that bitch Principal Callahan for getting us suspended for those games—but nobody could get the girl to talk. I can't believe she looks like she does now."

Drake points to Wilson. "Agreed."

"I dunno," Hill chimes in, leaning back on the bench. "She was too shy for me. I like my ladies wild. Loose."

"I'll take virgin pussy over loose pussy any day." Drake takes a swig from the beer bottle he's clutching. "What about you, Schwartz? Ever wanna fuck Frankie Callahan?"

My jaw begins to ache from clenching my teeth so hard and I work to school my features, because there is no way I'm about to let these morons in on what transpired between me and Frank.

I don't answer his asinine question, instead pushing myself from the booth and standing over the end of the table, glowering down at the idiots before me and wondering how I was ever friends with such dickbags.

"I think I better get going."

"What? Bailing so soon?" Wilson asks.

"Yep. I'm meeting some friends."

"Anyone we know?"

"Actually, yeah, and I just want to clear the air about something real quick." I lean down, pressing my hands on the table. All three guys gather closer like I'm about to spew some deep, dark secret. "If I ever—and I mean fucking *ever*—hear any of you washed-up, sorry sacks of shit talk about Frankie Callahan again, I'll staple your balls to a tree stump in the middle of the fucking town so everyone can see how small your dicks really are."

They all stare up at me, stunned into silence.

"And one last thing… I bet Julian Schenn can suck a mean cock. I'm sure you can ask your dads for confirmation." I tap the table twice. "Fun chatting with you all."

Without another glance in their direction, I make my way to Julian and Frankie's booth.

"Hey, guys. Sorry I'm late."

Slice Six

FRANKIE

"Did you just tell those morons I suck their dads' dicks?"

Julian's stare is enough to send most men cowering.

But not Jonas.

He stares back, unaffected. "Yep."

His bravery stirs something in me I haven't felt in far too long.

Desire.

I haven't been a complete saint since my first sexual encounter, but I also haven't gone all the way with anyone except Jonas. Don't get me wrong, I've had plenty of opportunities to—college boys are insanely horny—but it just never felt right with anyone else. I didn't feel anything close to what I felt with Jonas.

I'm not willing to sacrifice my feelings just to get off.

Julian cracks a smile, looking mighty proud of himself. "Well, you're not entirely wrong."

"What!" I croak, whacking his arm in disbelief. "You didn't tell me that! Who? Which one?"

"Dr. Drake." Julian licks his lips. "And he's hung."

"You little…little…"

"Whore?" His grin widens. "Guilty." He motions toward the empty side of the booth. "Have a seat, Jonas. We ordered waters for now."

There's a second where Jonas hesitates, but he shakes it off, sliding into the booth with grace.

"Thanks for inviting me out. It's nice to catch up with old friends."

A snort escapes me, and all eyes are trained on my face.

"Something to say, Frank?" Jonas gets straight to the point.

My palms itch, the urge to reach across the table and wipe the smug smile off his face strong.

But I can't.

"Well, for starters, *I* didn't invite you. I'd be just fine with never seeing your face again." *Lies.* "Also, I have an issue with the word friend. We aren't friends, Jonas. We never have been."

I don't know what I expected to come of the tongue-lashing. I wanted to hit him where it hurts in the best way I could, maybe even make him get angry.

But the last thing I ever expected—and I mean the very last thing—was for Jonas to throw his head back in laugher like what I said is the funniest thing he's heard in ages.

I also didn't anticipate being hit so hard with longing.

When I first saw him yesterday, I was angry. Bitter.

Though it didn't take long for me to feel the hole in my chest—that one I pretend doesn't exist—widen.

Now, seeing him laugh so freely—even at me—I feel it stretching bigger and bigger.

It makes me even angrier.

How dare he waltz back into my life with his stupid, sexy new beard that looks insanely lickable all trimmed up. That ridiculous ball cap pulled low over his green eyes. His muscles bigger and more defined than I've ever seen them before.

How fucking *dare* he make me feel things I haven't felt in years.

The pain. The anger. The...*tingles*.

Yesterday, after Julian left, I cried over Jonas Schwartz for the first time in four years.

I don't even know why I cried. It could have been that I'm still angry, that I'm annoyed by this hold he still has over me.

Or that it's clear to me I never stopped loving him.

No matter what it was, once the tears began flowing, it was impossible to get them to stop. Sleep eluded me, my mind racing in circles, and I'd be surprised if I managed a whopping three straight hours. My eyes were still swollen from crying and lack of sleep when I walked into work with Julian's beloved donuts clutched in my hand, chin held high as I tried to pretend everything was okay with me. He didn't say a word when he spotted me, just accepted his donuts and wrapped his arms around me as if he knew what was going on in my head and heart.

I loved him a little more in that moment.

Until he told me that even though I obviously spent the entire night reminiscing and trying to scheme up a way to get out of it, I was going for drinks tonight whether I liked it or not.

Then he brought up how he saved me from that Wilson guy perving on me at the store the other day, and drinks were back on.

Now, here I am, sitting across from Jonas.

The guy who took my virginity.

The guy who broke me.

The guy who can still make me cry all these years later.

The guy who makes my heart race, even when he's laughing at my own stupid words.

"Oh, Frank." He laughs, leaning across the table, encroaching on my space, making me feel smaller than I already am. "You kill me. Everyone at this table knows you and I were *much* more than friends."

Heat covers my cheeks and I sink into the booth, mortified even though he's right. We all know what happened between the two of us; I'd just rather not have my mistakes acknowledged out loud. It makes the bitter pill easier to swallow that way.

"Well, since we're apparently already playing with fire tonight, how about a shot or two of cinnamon whiskey? My treat."

Julian doesn't give either of us a chance to answer, scurrying off to the bar to place the order.

For the first time in four years, Jonas and I are alone.

Cue heart attack.

I drop my gaze to my lap, but I can feel Jonas raking his eyes over me. I hate it and love it at the same time.

My mind screams, *Don't react!* when I feel him shift in his seat and stretch out his long legs, his knee brushing against mine ever so slightly.

I don't move.

I don't breathe.

For those few minutes, we just exist.

He stares. I hide.

It's high school all over again.

We sit in silence like this for several minutes, and it takes me that long to realize Julian isn't coming back any time soon.

The waiter drops off our waters, and I almost beg him to stay forever and ever so I never have to sit alone with Jonas like this ever again.

Sweat begins to form on the backs of my knees, and I'm

beginning to stick to the booth.

I need to move or else I'm going to melt from nerves.

I scoot to the outer edge of the seat and peek around the corner, trying to get Julian's attention, but I know there's no use when I see him unabashedly flirting with the bartender.

As if he can feel my eyes on him, he turns toward me and winks then resumes his conversation.

Traitor.

"We've been ditched, haven't we?"

I startle at the sudden noise inside the otherwise quiet booth.

Jonas has the decency to look sorry.

Scooting back over to my spot—because, if I'm being honest, I miss the feel of his jeans rubbing against my bare legs—I frown. "Afraid so."

"What to talk about...what to talk about," he mutters, racking his brain for anything to say.

I should probably go with something safe. Something that won't set me off. Something that won't make him look like the bad guy.

Screw that.

I fold my hands together and lean against the table, pursing my lips.

"Gee, Jonas, what should we talk about first? Should we discuss you pretending to like me and stringing me along for months? Maybe that time I *finally* gained enough courage—after months and months of pep talks and practiced conversations in my head—to invite you to do something *other* than write in those stupid notebooks of yours and you let me down?" I slap my hand against my head. "Wait, I'm remembering that wrong. First you *laid* me down and let me give you something you *knew* meant *everything* to me. *Then* you broke my heart and refused to ever speak to me again. *That's* what happened." I hold my hand up when he opens his mouth. "No, no, you're right. That's all too silly. Let's talk about the weather. Definitely the weather."

He sits there, mouth dropped open, eyes full of surprise.

Good. I've shocked him—just like he shocked me by leaving me. You know what they say about turnabout...it's fair play.

I wrap my hand around my water, taking a long pull of the cool liquid, watching Jonas over the rim of the glass.

His green eyes, which were shining bright when he first walked up, are growing darker and darker as the seconds tick away.

I glance up, checking to make sure the lightbulb hanging above us isn't short-circuiting.

It's just fine.

I look back at Jonas.

He's *fuming.*

"I don't know what pisses me off more, Frank—the fact that you think I faked *any* of what we exchanged in our notebooks, or that you think I'm pathetic enough to string a girl like you along for *months* all in hopes of *maybe* scoring. Or maybe I'm mad at myself for not realizing how damn self-centered you are for not stopping to think for one second that I was hurting too."

He was hurting?

"What the hell do you mean by 'a girl like me'? What do you mean *you* were hurting? You had no right to hurt. *You*"—I stab a finger his way—"left *me.*" I point at my chest, at my heart, the biggest thing he left behind.

"You ate lunch in the library and firmly believed in doing homework over the weekends. You were meek. You hid." He chuckles sardonically, bringing his glass up and downing half of it in an easy chug. "I was the captain of a state-championship-winning football team, for crying out loud. All I had to do was wave my fingers and I could have had any person in that school. *That's* what I meant by a girl like you." He leans across the table again. "I didn't *have* to talk to you,

77

Frankie. I fucking wanted to."

"I—"

"I'm not finished," he snaps, cutting me off.

I don't back down. I don't let his anger intimidate me.

I'm happy he's mad. Being mad is better than the silence I've gotten in the last four years.

"Do you truly think all I did was play you? So, what, I got what I wanted from you—what you think I wanted—then just booked it out of there and never spoke to you again? Mind you, *you* were the one who threw yourself at me. I never asked for what you gave me. You made that choice all on your own before you even uttered an invitation and you know that."

He's right.

I made the choice to give Jonas my virginity long before I worked up the courage to invite him over. We shared a connection because of those notebooks. They were a way for us to share everything about ourselves that we never had the nerve to say out loud.

Like how, while he loved his father and was proud of his accomplishments, Jonas didn't want to be like him, counting every penny to get through until the next paycheck.

He wanted security.

He had dreams—big dreams—and he wasn't going to let anything stand in his way.

"Besides, I didn't have a choice in leaving you. I had to."

"Yeah, for your scholarship. We all had to leave for college eventually, Jonas. I'm not upset about that." I roll my eyes. "I'm upset about you leaving me before you actually left town."

"You're not getting it, Frank. I had to leave you then too."

"No, you didn't. You *chose* to."

"I didn't choose shit. Ask your father."

My brows shoot up. I must have heard him wrong. "Excuse me?"

"I said, ask your father."

"My father has nothing to do with this," I scoff, annoyed because now he's just playing games.

Jonas tosses his head back, loud obnoxious laughter ringing through the bar.

I blink at him and his antics.

He has officially gone insane.

There is no way my father had anything to do with what happened between us. It's not possible. Jonas snuck out of the house before my parents even made it inside. They had no idea he was ever there. I was careful.

Jonas is lying.

Sobering, he wipes at his eyes, shaking his head.

He levels me with a stare, and there's this hardness in his gaze I've never seen before.

"Oh, Frank. He has everything to do with this."

A tray full of shots is plopped down on the table, and I glance up to see a grinning Julian.

"Here, you two sound like you need these."

Without a word, Jonas grabs a shot and tosses it back.

I down one too.

He takes another, and so do I.

We're each three shots in before Julian slips into the booth, eyes darting between the two of us.

"Looks like you two were mighty thirsty. Good thing I got here when I did."

He laughs at his joke.

We don't.

Jonas and I sit there, locked in a stare-down, neither one of us willing to lose this battle.

I don't know if it's the alcohol or the way he keeps dropping his gaze to my lips that's making me feel buzzed, but either way, I'm starting to feel things I know I shouldn't.

Drop, flick.

Drop, flick.

He shifts, his leg firmly planted against my own. He knows what he's doing. He's not stupid.

In school, he'd find a way to touch me every day. A simple brush of our elbows, our knees, or he'd walk extra close to me, his chest rubbing against my back. It didn't matter how small it was; I felt it everywhere.

He knew.

Just like he knows now that the pressure between my legs, the pressure I've felt since I walked inside and laid eyes on him, is building.

I want to crawl across the table and sit myself in his lap.

I want him between my legs. I want his mouth against my neck, my shoulder, my lips.

I want to feel him everywhere again.

Julian clears his throat, and I'm thrown from the haze that's settled around me.

"So, what'd I miss?"

I knew trying to keep up with Jonas was a big mistake.

He's downed three more shots, and despite devouring nearly an entire basket of mozzarella sticks, I'm feeling it.

I'm not drunk, but I am buzzing pretty hard.

Which is probably why, like a complete idiot, I agreed to share a ride home with my nemesis.

"You sure you're okay riding home with him?" Julian asks for the fifth time.

I nod. "It just makes sense. We live close to one another. You live on the other side of town with all the other rich kids who still live with their parents."

"Oooh, drunk Frankie is mean Frankie. I'll have to make a note of that."

"One, I'm not drunk. And two"—I poke his nose—"*boop*. You still love me."

Laughing, he wraps me in a warm hug. "I do still love you. Just make good choices, Frankie. You have a weakness when it comes to him."

"You have nothing to worry about. Anything I had with Jonas is long past."

"You're drunk and, seeing as you're agreeing to share a cab with him, obviously already not thinking clearly."

"Buzzed," I insist.

"Either way, be smart."

"Yes, Dad." I squeeze him. "Thanks for giving me a night out. I needed it. I mean, inviting Jonas was a dick move, but thank you."

Our cab pulls up and Julian releases me. He walks over to Jonas, and the two shake hands. I see their lips move, but I can't make out what either of them are saying.

Julian gives me one last wave, walking backward toward his car. "Night, Frankenstein."

"Night, Igor."

I gulp in a deep breath, gathering the strength I need to make it through this ride, and turn toward the cab.

Jonas holds open the door for me. "Frankenstein, huh?"

I huff, walking around to the other side, ignoring his gesture. "It's a hell of a lot better than what you came up with."

His eyes smile at me over the top of the cab. "I'll be the judge of that, *Frank*."

We climb inside and I rattle off my address to the driver then begin telling him we'll be making another stop at Jonas' house.

"No we won't," he interrupts.

"Uh, yes we will."

"I'll walk from your house."

"Jonas, it'll be midnight by the time we get to my place, and you live almost a mile away. Don't be stupid."

"I'm not being stupid. I want the fresh air."

"Fine." I huff. "Suit yourself."

Then, it's quiet again.

Our go-to.

Despite our arguing earlier, I actually had a good time tonight.

Hanging out with Jonas wasn't so bad when Julian was there.

I guess that's our issue—we can't be alone together.

We're either fucking or fighting, and since we definitely aren't fucking right now, fighting it is.

"Your voice sounds different than it used to."

"The more I drink, the deeper it gets. I've been spending a lot of my time drinking lately."

Despite how I feel about Jonas and the way he left me, my heart aches at the thought of him losing the one thing he loved most in this world—the game.

Even though we didn't attend the same college, the art institute I attended was an affiliate of his school and our campus claimed his football team as our own. By the morning after the game, everyone was talking about his fall and the repercussions—a shattered kneecap and his NFL career put on an indefinite hold.

"Why'd you climb the bleachers, Jonas?"

He sighs heavily, sinking back into the seat, closing his eyes, and rubbing at his temples.

"You don't have to tell me."

Miles pass by before he says anything again, and the only sound in the quiet cab is the soft melody of some folk song drifting through the speakers.

"Do you want the story I've been feeding everyone for months or the actual reason?"

My mouth drops open at the offer.

I'm stunned.

Not that he's been lying to everyone—Jonas proved he's a snake a long time ago—but that he'd give me of all people the real story behind his literal fall from grace.

"You'd give that to me?"

"Sure. You won't believe me, but I'll tell you."

"Why wouldn't I believe you?"

"Because it involves you."

Slice Seven

JONAS

"We're here."

She hasn't said anything for the last two miles.

I don't know if it's shock or maybe that she just didn't hear me.

I pull out enough cash to cover the bill and a tip, sliding it into the cabbie's waiting hand. "Thanks, Leroy," I say.

"I'm sure I'll see ya later this week, Jonas."

I try not to cringe at his statement.

Since I've been back, I've spent a few too many nights roaming the streets, running and walking until my knee wants to give out. I call Leroy, the only cabbie in town, for a ride back home more often than I'd like to.

I roll out of the cab, rounding the car and pulling Frankie's door open for her.

"Bull," she says as she slides out and brushes past me.

"Chicken."

"Huh?"

"Oh." I close the cab door and face her as Leroy pulls away from us. "I thought we were just naming random animals. Is that not what we're doing?"

"Why would we just name random animals, Jonas?"

I scrub a hand over my face. "I don't know, Frank. I'm tired and a little drunk. I can't think straight around you as it is. I'm not sure why I thought it was a good idea to add alcohol into the mix."

"I'm thankful for the liquid courage," she murmurs. "It makes me brave."

"It's nothing but a Band-Aid for everything wrong in my life."

Her brows pinch together, and I want to reach over and smooth the crinkles between them.

"What happened, Jonas?" She takes a step toward me, and I'm not even sure she realizes she's moving closer with every word. "What do I have to do with any of it?"

If I wanted to, I could reach out and touch her right now.

I want to.

I really, *really* want to.

"I saw you," I blurt.

Her mocha eyes widen for a split second when she realizes she's been busted, but she spares us both the awkwardness and doesn't deny being at my games.

I can't hold back any longer.

I reach for her, wrapping a single hand around her waist and pulling her small frame against me. She lets me, like she's just been waiting for me to give in to the desire.

Just like I knew she would, she still fits against me like she was made to be there.

Leaving one hand dangling at my side, I rest my chin against her temple and breathe in the sweet orange scent I've missed for far too long. She places her hands against my chest, sinking into me and keeping me away all at once.

I've fucking missed this.

I want to wrap both arms around her and pull her against me until there's not a single breath of space between our bodies.

I want to sweep my hands down her curves, feel her ass fill my palms.

I want to lift her mouth to mine and kiss her until neither of us can feel our lips.

But none of that is mine to have anymore, so I don't press for more.

We stand there like that, my hand on her waist, her body angled toward mine, my chin resting against her head.

We're not quite embracing, but we're not standing with a field of all our mistakes separating us either.

We're meeting at the 50-yard line together.

"How many times were you there?"

"E-Enough to know why the NFL wanted you as badly as I did."

I sigh. "Why were you there, Frank? Why did you come to my games?"

"Because I wanted to see you."

"Why didn't you ever tell me?"

She laughs dryly, and I feel her body shake against mine. "I was angry, Jonas."

"Are you still angry?"

"Yes."

No hesitation from her, and the reality that Frankie could never be mine socks me right in the gut.

"Are you always going to be angry?"

She doesn't answer right away, and I gulp, my stomach rolling with anticipation.

Or maybe that's from the alcohol.

I don't know at this point.

"I don't know."

It's all I need.

I grin against her soft skin. "So you're saying there's a chance?"

She laughs, shoving away from me, taking two steps back and putting that distance back between us.

A distance I'd happily sprint, broken knee and all.

I shove my thumb over my shoulder. "I better head home. I told my parents not to wait up, but they don't listen for shit."

She nods but doesn't say anything else.

"I'll see you around."

Another nod.

I take two steps backward, hoping she'll take the cue and walk inside, but she doesn't. She just stands there, looking off past my shoulder but not really staring at anything in particular.

It's like she's lost in memories of the past, and I wish we could both go back there. I'd do so many things so differently.

"I wasn't there that night."

Her words stop me, and my heart seizes when her eyes collide with mine. She looks so...sad. She looks sorry.

"I wasn't there. I had tickets, but I also had an interview I couldn't miss. There was no way I could have made it back in time."

Shoving my hands into my pockets so I don't reach for her again and try to soothe away the sadness radiating off her, I nod. "I know."

"But that's why you climbed the bleachers. You thought you saw me. Right?"

"I saw you at the previous game—I'd know those curls anywhere—and I scoured the stands for you at the bowl game. I thought there was no way you'd miss it. There was a girl with wild curls, and the light hit them just right. I was so certain it was you. So, I jumped. I took the chance. I called your name, but you didn't turn around. The realization that you weren't there knocked me on my ass."

"Literally." Her lips twitch. "Sorry. Too soon probably."

I can't help but laugh. "I kind of miss you giving me shit."

"Someone's gotta do it."

"Well," I say, rocking back on my heels. "Good night, Frank."

We don't move.

"You're not leaving," she says quietly.

"Because I don't want to. Also, because I'm waiting for you to walk inside. I'm not leaving you standing in the middle of the sidewalk."

"Oh," she squeaks. "Right. Well, bye."

She darts off up the stairs and toward her apartment building.

Just as she pulls open the door, she looks back at me.

I tilt my head in a silent question. She chews on her bottom lip, like she's trying to bite back whatever it is she wants to say.

She shakes her head, and I know I'm not getting anything else out of her tonight.

"Good night, Jonas."

She disappears inside, and for what feels like the millionth time, I want to kick myself for ever believing her father's threats and letting her go.

I might be back in town because of my bum knee, but it's not the only thing I need to fix.

Slice Eight

FRANKIE

I've concluded something is wrong with me.

I've ordered from Slice four times since Jonas left me at my apartment, just trying to catch a glimpse of him, but he hasn't delivered to me once.

I don't know why I want to see him. I'm still angry.

But I also miss him. I miss how easy everything is between us. Well, how easy it *used* to be.

Now I'm turned on by our sparring.

Ugh. Maybe I just need to masturbate to him and get it over with. Over the last week, I've found myself sliding my hand into my panties too many times, always pulling away before I finish.

I don't know if I'm punishing myself for wanting him, or if I'm just insane.

Since I'm currently on hold waiting to place yet another order,

I'm going with insane.

"Thank you for calling Slice. This is Drew, how can I help you?"

"Hi, Drew, it's me again."

I hear a soft laugh. "Hey, Frankie. Want your usual?"

My face heats because I know she knows there's a reason for me ordering so much.

"Yes, please. Can, uh, can I ask you something?"

"Shoot." There's a loud ruckus in the background on her end of the line, and Drew sighs heavily. "Mother of—Winston Daniels! I swear to all things holy, I am going to put my entire foot up your giant ass!"

"Quit looking at my ass, Woods!"

"That's it—I'm killing you now. Frankie, I'll put your order in. Give us fifteen and we'll have it there."

The line goes dead, just like Winston is about to be.

Laughing, I toss my cell aside and retrieve my charcoal pencil—my medium of the week—rolling it through my fingers and staring down at the piece I'm currently working on.

There's something familiar about the face I'm drawing, but I can't place it.

I let my fingers continue to work anyway, trying to quiet the voices in my head.

Last night, I had my weekly dinner with my parents. To say it was a disaster would be an understatement.

My mom asked if I had been up to anything fun lately, so I told her about going out with Julian and Jonas. The moment I said his name, the wine glass that was perched in her hand went crashing to the floor.

My father didn't speak to me for the rest of the night.

It was strange, and it didn't strengthen my argument of my father is innocent.

I'm so lost in my mind, I nearly throw my sketchpad across the room when the doorbell chimes.

"Son of a holy shit, Batman!"

There's a chuckle on the other side of the door as I push myself up off the couch, tossing my pencil and pad onto the cushion beside me.

"Hey, Brad," I say, pulling open the door and reaching into my clutch. "How you doing tonight?"

"Two things. One, 'son of a holy shit, Batman'? I've never heard that one before. Two, I am most definitely not Brad."

My lips pop open. "Jonas?"

"In the flesh."

"I-I-I…" I clear my throat and push my shoulders back. "I wasn't expecting you. It's usually Brad."

"Usually, huh? Have you been ordering from Slice a lot?"

Red rushes into my cheeks. "No more than normal," I lie.

"Whatever you say." He grins wolfishly, and I love the way his smile sits against his beard. "I've got a pie for ya. Drew also threw in an order of cheese sticks as an apology for Winston's behavior."

"She's the best."

"She's something, that's for sure."

Cue awkward silence.

Now that I have him in front of me, I have no idea what I want to say.

Not that I wanted to say anything to begin with.

I think, maybe, I just missed him.

"So…"

"So…" he echoes.

"Can I have my pizza?"

"Right." Jonas pulls open the insulated bag and slides out my pie with ease. "I suppose that is technically why I'm here."

"Technically?"

"I saw your name come up on the board and I paid Brad to take it."

"You paid him? Isn't that sort of counterproductive on your part since you work for tips?"

"Well, yeah, but I'm me." His grin turns cocky. "I'll make up for it."

I should have known that'd be the case. I'm certain the local pizzeria, which is already mega-popular, has seen a big boom in business with *the* Jonas Schwartz back in town. Everyone loves their local celebrity too much not to roll the dice to see if he'll deliver.

Jonas seems a little embarrassed to be back here and not in the NFL, but his hometown is eating it up in the best of ways.

"Why did you want to take it?"

He raises his brows. "Is that a serious question?"

"I wouldn't have asked if I knew the answer."

"Because I wanted to see you, Frank."

My heart swells at his confession.

"Today was my first day back this week and I was secretly watching the board all night to see if your address would pop up."

"First day back?"

He nods. "I had some meetings with my agent and doctor upstate."

"Any news on your recovery?"

It would be subtle to most, but being somebody who watched Jonas every day for an entire school year, I see a spark in his eye.

"There's improvement, but I'm not quite ready for the field just yet."

"Improvement is good though."

"It definitely is."

He shifts around, like he's uncomfortable with the conversation.

Or just tired of standing there holding my pizza.

"Here. Let me take that."

He pulls the box back. "Not so fast. This is my bargaining chip."

"Come again?"

Lifting the pie, he says, "I'm holding this hostage until you let me in."

Let him in? Like, inside my apartment?

I was wrong. I'm not insane.

He is.

"Don't you have to work?"

"Ah, that's where things get fun. I'm off the clock."

My brows pinch together, not understanding. "You're delivering this on your own time?"

"I am."

For the first time since I opened the door, I'm noticing he's not wearing his normal *Slice, Slice Baby* shirt.

"Why?"

"I wanted to see you."

He says it like it's the most logical answer in the entire world.

There's a heavy pause. He steps toward me, the scent that's all Jonas filling my senses. I clutch the doorframe until my knuckles turn white to keep myself from reaching for him.

"Invite me inside, Frank."

"I want to."

"Then do it."

"I'm scared."

His lips tilt up. "I'll only kiss you if you ask me to."

Now I'm white-knuckling the doorway because if I don't hold on to something, I'm certain I'll be a puddle on the floor.

"Frank?"

I don't say anything. I can't.

Instead, I take a step to the side.

He grins and pushes past me.

I try not to let my heart burst out of my chest.

The door clicks shut behind me, the sound deafening in my otherwise quiet apartment.

Jonas stands just inside the door, unmoving.

I grab the pizza from his hands and lead us into the living room, setting the pie down on the coffee table.

"Want some pizza? I'll grab plates."

Before he can say anything, I rush off to the kitchen.

I wrench open the freezer door and practically shove my head inside, needing a moment to cool off—*literally*.

Jonas is inside my apartment.

I invited him in.

I *want* him here.

What is going on with me? I'm supposed to be mad at him, not inviting him into my home.

Am I *that* desperate for attention? Or does he just make me that weak?

"Are you trying to move into that thing or something? I can bring you a pillow if you'd like."

I jump at Jonas' sudden appearance, whacking my head on the freezer shelf.

"Crap!" I clutch my throbbing head. "Mother of Merlin, that hurt!"

"Shit," he mutters, rushing forward. His big palm wraps around my waist and tugs me close to him. "Let me see it."

"Is it bleeding? Am I going to bleed out? How much blood is there?"

He chuckles, moving my hand out of the way. "I can't tell if you're worried about blood or not."

"Shut up!" I swat at him. "I hate blood. I can't look. I can't look or I'll puke. It's the worst. It's—*oh god*, I can *smell* it. It's bad, isn't it?"

"You're nuts. The only bad thing is your sense of smell because you definitely *aren't* bleeding."

"Then how come I can taste it!"

"We've just established that you're insane."

I try to pull away from him, but he doesn't let me get far.

"Okay, okay. Fine," he says, pulling me back in until my body molds against his. I try not to sigh at the contact. "You're not insane. You're just..." He shakes his head. "Yeah, no, I lied. You're insane."

"Jonas!"

"Just accept it. The sooner you do, the better off you'll be."

"I'm going to knee you in the balls." There's no bite behind my scolding. Being in his arms has rendered me stupid.

He laughs because he knows exactly what he's doing just by touching me. "You'd never hurt my balls."

"Ah, that's where you're wrong. You think just because we've slung back a few shots together and I've invited you into my apartment, you're forgiven, but you are incorrect. I'm still plenty angry with you, Jonas."

He tightens his hold, lips dropping to my ear, dangerously close to tracing the shell.

My shirt has ridden up, and his warm fingers graze over my skin, leaving a path of fire in their wake.

I shiver at the touch, and he chuckles, his chest vibrating against me.

"You know, I'm beginning to think it's not anger you harbor toward me, Frank." Another squeeze. "I think you're just sexually frustrated."

He's wrong. I am still angry.

But...if I'm being honest, he's right too.

I *am* sexually frustrated.

No matter how many times I tried in college, nobody could make me feel the way Jonas does.

I'll either end up a spinster chasing a high I've only experienced once before, or I'll give in to him, which doesn't bode well for me either way you look at it.

Though one way does sound a hell of a lot more fun…

Like he can read my thoughts, he presses his hips against me, and it's clear I'm not the only one who is sexually frustrated.

I groan at the contact, my head falling back and lolling to the side.

His nose is cold against my skin, but I love the feel as he drags it along the column of my neck.

"Oranges."

"Oranges?"

"You still smell like oranges." His tongue sneaks out, tasting me. "But you don't taste like oranges."

A moan escapes my lips, and I hate the way my body betrays me, giving away the effect he has on me.

"How's your head?"

"What head?"

He laughs against my skin, and the vibrations run through me and straight between my legs.

"The one you just hurt."

"Oh. It's fine. I've already forgotten all about it."

"So you're not concussed?" He blazes a path from my neck to my cheek, switching between open- and close-mouthed kisses.

I squeeze my legs together, trying to alleviate some of the pressure that's steadily building there.

"No."

Another kiss. A flick of his tongue.

"No emergency room visit necessary?"

He's dangerously close to my lips.

"No."

"You're thinking clearly?"

No, but I never think clearly around you. "Yes."

"Then ask me."

Kiss me.

The words sit on the tip of my tongue, but I can't seem to make myself say them.

I want to. God, do I want to.

But I can't.

Asking Jonas to kiss me is like asking him to break my heart all over again.

I won't give him that power.

Instead, I press onto my tiptoes and crush my mouth against his.

He wasn't expecting it, but it doesn't take long before his hands weave through my hair and he's holding me to him, taking control of the kiss.

Suddenly, everything feels right again.

The way he cradles my head, how his new beard feels scraping my chin. The way his chest brushes against mine. His tongue sweeping into my mouth.

It's all so right.

Everything I've been missing and more.

He pulls back, sighing as he rests his forehead on mine. "I've missed this. So much."

I nod, because I can't form words right now.

"I've missed you, Frank."

Nod.

"I'm sorry I left the way I did."

Another nod.

"Please stop being mad at me."

I don't answer.

I kiss him again.

Jonas lets me.

One hand remains in my hair as the other trails down my back, down and down and down until he's cupping my ass.

Without much effort, he lifts me off the ground, and I wrap my legs around his waist.

For a moment, I worry about his knee and all the extra weight, but I push the thought aside. Jonas knows his body and his limits.

I trust him.

The reality of the thought hits me.

Even after everything, I still trust him.

Just not with my heart. Not yet, at least.

He walks us backward until I'm resting on top of the counter and he's between my legs. His fingers snake under my shirt until his hand is precariously close to my breast.

I know he feels my heart rate pick up, anticipating his touch, because I feel him smile against me.

He kisses his way over my chin, down my neck, and across my collarbone until he's trailed a path to my chest.

My nipples pebble, and I want nothing more than for him to close his mouth around me and help ease some of this pressure between my legs.

"Can I?"

"Can you? Good gravy, Jonas, take my damn shirt off already!"

Laughing, he pulls the material from my body, leaving me sitting atop the counter in nothing but my bra and tiny sleep shorts.

He stares down at my chest, and there's an unmistakable hunger in his eyes.

"Do you need instructions?"

Jonas smirks at my smartass comment. "Well, this is quite the turn from the first time we did this."

"The first time we did this, I didn't know what I wanted, and everything felt amazing."

"Maybe I was just that good."

You were. "Just touch me, Jonas."

With shaking fingers, he pulls the cups of my bra down, the pads of his thumbs grazing over my sensitive nipples.

I'm not sure if it's his touch that makes me tremble, or if it's the fact that he's as nervous as I am.

"Perfect," he mutters. "So fucking perfect."

Lowering his head, he flicks his tongue out, teasing me. I growl in disapproval and he laughs, closing his mouth around me, letting the vibrations quiver through me.

"Oh holy… *Wow.*"

He pulls away. "See? Told you I know what I'm doing."

"Well then don't stop!"

He doesn't.

I don't know how long we spend on the counter, Jonas giving each breast the attention it deserves. I'm writhing, looking for even the smallest amount of friction where I need it.

"Touch yourself, Frank."

"Like…in front of you?"

He chuckles. "Yes."

My heart begins to hammer for other reasons.

I've never touched myself in front of someone before. I've always left that for late at night when everyone else is asleep, no one around to hear my moans.

But I'm aching. I need relief.

Swallowing, I say, "I will if you will."

He nods, dropping one hand to the button on his jeans and working it open. The sound of his zipper is loud, the rustling of his hand as he frees himself deafening.

Unlike all those years ago, I don't look away as he pulls himself from his jeans.

He wraps his fist around his length, working his erection in a slow rhythm as he stares down at me.

Stepping away until he's no longer touching me, he leans forward a bit. "Fair is fair, Frank."

I swallow the lump in my throat and slide my hand inside my shorts, but he shakes his head, stopping me.

"W-What?"

"Pull your shorts to the side. Spread your legs for me so I can see."

His words push me nearer to the edge I'm already close to slipping over.

With an encouraging deep breath, I follow his request, pulling my skimpy bottoms aside and stretching my legs wide.

At first it feels strange being exposed to him like this, but seeing the fire dancing in his green eyes and watching his cock jump, I feel sexy.

Brave.

Wanted.

"Son of a bitch," he mutters. His eyes flash to mine with a realization. "You're not wearing any underwear."

I shake my head. "I sleep naked." Shrug. "Seemed pointless to put them on after my shower."

"One leg up on the counter."

I obey.

"Scoot forward."

I do.

"Now touch yourself."

Slowly, I drag my fingers over my shaved mound and trace a

single digit over my swollen clit.

His eyes flare again, and he grips his cock tighter, biting at his lip.

I add another finger and begin to rub short, slow circles over my bud, my own eyes glued to what he's doing to himself.

I'm not focused on what I must look like to him, spread wide on the counter. All I'm thinking about is how I feel.

And right now, I feel like I'm going to explode.

I slide a single finger into my hole, and Jonas stutters in his movements.

I add another.

"Fucking hell," he whispers with a gravelly voice.

He takes a step closer, reaching out for me. I watch as his fingertips dance along my inner thigh and down, down, down, inching closer and closer to just where I want him.

His gaze meets mine, and his Adam's apple bobs heavily as he swallows. "I need to touch you."

I don't say anything, and I don't break eye contact.

A single finger grazes against my clit, and I come undone with the simple touch.

"Oh shit," he drawls out, and then his mouth is on mine, like he can't stand to not touch me.

He wraps my hair around his hand, his grip so hard it almost hurts. He pulls me to him roughly, fitting himself between my legs once again, and I go to him with eagerness.

"I need to be inside you again."

I moan. "Please."

"Do you have anything? I wasn't planning on this."

"I..." Crap. "N-No. I, uh, I've never had a reason to have anything."

He pulls back, looking at me with pinched brows. Then, his eyes widen.

"Frank, have...have you been with anyone since me?"

I'm flaming red right now, and it's not from the orgasm I just had. I shake my head. "Not all the way."

"Fuck," he mutters, scrubbing a hand over his face. "We can't do this."

"What?" I nearly cry out. "What do you mean?"

"I mean, we can't do this. We rushed it last time. We can't rush it again."

"We didn't rush it. I wanted it then and I want it now."

"Come on, Frankie. You know we rushed it. You know it wasn't what you wanted your first time to be—a hurried romp and me splitting before our bodies even came down from the high."

His words hit me like a bucket of cold water, reminding me that Jonas Schwartz isn't just good at playing football.

He's good at playing hearts.

And he played mine.

"I don't want to rush this, Frankie. I want to savor it."

I'm hurt by his rejection and a little embarrassed, but deep down, I know he's right.

I always jump in heart first when it comes to him, and this time, I need to use my head. I don't want this time with Jonas to be another thing I look back on and wish had gone differently.

I want it to be perfect.

I slide my legs off the counter, moving back to a seated position. "You're right."

"I am?"

I glare at him. "I'm not repeating it."

He smirks. "Fine. Can't blame me for trying though." He pecks a kiss to my forehead. "Look, not to seem like a dick or anything, but I think it's probably best if I head home. Clearly we can't be trusted to be alone together right now."

A Slice of Love

"Clearly." I laugh. "Yeah, you're right. You should go." I look pointedly at his still-hard dick. "You could probably go for a shower right about now."

"A very, very cold shower."

He tucks himself away as best he can, and I can't help but grin at the tent in his shorts, which is still painfully obvious.

He looks down and shrugs, not ashamed of his arousal at all.

When he glances back to me, I'm surprised to find his eyes glowing with happiness.

"You're not mad?"

"No? Should I be?"

"Well, I don't know. You're leaving."

"It was my idea," he reminds me. "Besides, I got to watch you get off. That's going to take up the bulk of my spank bank for quite some time."

"Just the bulk?"

"I'm sorry, have you *seen* Scar Jo?"

I laugh. "Fair enough."

Jonas steps toward me again. His hand coming up to cup my jaw, he brings my eyes to his.

"Thank you for tonight."

"Shouldn't I be the one thanking you?"

"Spank bank." He drops his mouth to mine in a quick, tame kiss, and I miss him the moment he pulls away.

I'm going to miss him doubly when I finally get my heart rate to settle down and I'm tucked into bed alone.

He brushes his nose against mine, the touch so intimate it surprises me.

"Good night, Frank."

"Good night, Jonas."

Slice Nine

JONAS

It's been less than twenty-four hours since I last saw Frankie, and I have something I need to prove to myself—can we spend time together that doesn't end in an argument or sex?

Hence why I'm standing outside her apartment with my version of an apology: food.

What exactly I'm apologizing for, I'm not certain.

I just know I feel bad for last night.

Mostly for my own balls, but also for turning Frankie down.

She might have gotten off, but it was clear she wanted more. I did too, but the last time we let things go too far, nothing ended the right way.

I have another shot with her, and I'm not going to screw it up this time.

Sure, the screwup last time was mostly on her father's part, but also mine. I was the dumbass kid who believed her father could ruin my football career with a few phone calls.

As it turned out, her father couldn't touch me, but I didn't realize that until it was too late and the damage had already been done.

Frankie wanted nothing to do with me, and I couldn't blame her.

Because I knew her parents wouldn't let me anywhere near her, I waited for our shot in college.

Only she never showed up, so I could never explain.

Before I knew it, four years flew by.

Now I have a chance to prove to her what she means to me, what she's always meant to me. I'm not about to let that chance pass me by.

I rap my knuckles against her door.

There's a rustling behind the wooden frame, and it reminds me of the first time I came here.

Never in a million years did I expect Frankie to be behind the door. I paid zero attention to the name on the order—not that it would have done me any good since all it said was Doctor Frankenstein, and that could have been anyone.

When I did realize it was her, I was floored.

Just as I am now when she swings the door open.

Frankie Callahan has always been beautiful, snagging my attention from the beginning, but she was shy. She hid behind her hair and her glasses and her books.

Now, she carries herself with a confidence that makes her stunning.

And it makes me all the more attracted to her.

"Jonas?"

"Frank!"

She pokes her head out, looking around the hallway. "What are you doing here?"

"I brought you dinner."

Her brows shoot up as she stares down at the box from Slice. "Why?"

"Because you need to eat."

"I can make my own dinner?"

"Is that a question or are you telling me?"

She huffs. "Telling you."

"Right." I shake the box. "I brought your favorite."

"My favorite? What exactly is my favorite?"

"A Slice of Love."

Her eyes light up, her plump lips pulling into a wide smile. "You brought me a slice of Molly Daniels' famous white chocolate strawberry cake?" I nod. "For dinner?"

"Yep."

"Well then why the hell are you still standing in the doorway? Get in here!"

She fists my shirt, pulling me inside her apartment. She snatches the box out of my hand, barreling toward the kitchen, suddenly on a mission.

"There are two forks in the box," I inform her.

"Two?" She barks out a laugh. "You're lucky you're cute, Jonas, because you'd make an awful comedian."

"So you think I'm cute, huh?"

"You brought me my favorite cake—of course you're cute."

"Why are you still headed for the kitchen?"

"I need milk!"

I follow her, shaking my head as she grabs a carton of chocolate milk—skipping the glass—and hops up onto the same counter I had her on top of just last night.

Leaning against the counter opposite her, my eyes are glued to the spot where she was spread open for me, fingers plunging deep into her pussy.

As if on cue, Frankie moans.

My dick twitches, a miracle considering how many times I got off last night conjuring up the same images and noises.

I reach down to adjust myself, and Frankie doesn't miss the movement.

"Stop thinking about sex. I'm trying to enjoy this moment."

"You say that like you wouldn't enjoy sex with me, which we both know is bullshit."

She blushes, and my cock jumps again.

"So, why are you really here, Jonas? It can't just be to bring me cake."

"What if it is?"

"Then you're lying."

"Ah, that's where you're wrong."

She pauses mid-bite. "Seriously?"

"Seriously."

"No ulterior motives?"

"Nope." I fold my arms over my chest. "Not a single one."

She eyes me like she doesn't believe me, and I sigh, motioning over my chest.

"Cross my heart, Frank. I'm just here for the friendship."

"Ah, yes, our scintillating conversation skills. How could I forget."

"You are the only human in the world who could use a word like scintillating in an everyday discussion and not have it sound weird."

"Thank you." She shovels another bite of cake into her mouth, washing it down with a drink of milk. "This is weird, you watching me."

"Well, I didn't intend to just watch you. I was supposed to be enjoying that cake with you, but *no*. Someone's stingy."

"Can you blame me? This cake is heaven. A literal slice of—"

"Love?" I provide.

She smiles. "Yes."

Her eyes flit to the box and she gasps. "No way!"

"Yes way."

Setting her cake to the side, she unsticks the composition notebook that's taped to the lid of the box and flips through the pages.

"It's empty." She frowns.

"Because we're going to fill it. Just like old times."

"Just like old times," she repeats quietly, running her fingers over the cover tentatively. "Is it weird that I'm nervous?"

"Why would you be nervous?"

"Because last time we did this, these notebooks lead to a lot of…um, big decisions. Are we ready for that again?"

Her eyes are pleading with me not to hurt her again. It sucks, but it's warranted.

"I'll meet you at the 50-yard line if you're game."

Hope sparks to life in her gaze, but it's the only hint I have as to whether she's truly up for this in a way that's beyond physical.

"I'm game."

Grinning, she sets the book aside and picks her cake back up, swinging her feet back and forth like she's never been more excited in her life.

Though I'm not sure if that's just the cake talking or because of the notebook, I'm hoping for the latter.

"So, how was your day?"

"Really? That's what you're going with?"

I nod. "Yes. How was your day?"

She looks skeptical that all I want is a simple conversation, and to be fair, if I were her, I'd be wary too.

But it's honestly all I'm here for.

"My day was…well, not too bad actually. It flew by, but I was able to knock out a good portion of my to-do list, including lunch with my father."

I do my best not to show any sort of reaction at the mention of him.

"How, uh, how are your parents?" I ask because I know it's expected.

"They're...well, to tell you the truth, we're struggling a bit."

"Oh?" Her brows lift as my voice jumps two octaves. I cough. "Sorry, swallowed wrong," I lie. "What's going on?"

She sighs heavily, setting her empty plate on the counter next to her. "For starters, my father has cancer."

"Cancer? Jesus fuck, Frank."

Her lips pull up on one side. "I don't think my father would appreciate that language very much."

I ignore her smartass comment. "I had no idea he was sick. How bad is it?"

"We just went to the doctor earlier this week. It's not any better, but it's not any worse right now. We're sort of in limbo with it. It could go either way."

"Shit. I know you're close with your parents."

"Was. I was close with them. I haven't been for years."

"What happened?"

She flicks her eyes my way. It's brief, but it's enough for me to know I have something to do with it.

"We wanted different things for my life and had a difficult time compromising. My mother came around first, but my father was a different story. We've only been speaking for six months now, since we found out about the cancer."

I cross the kitchen, not stopping until I've planted myself between her legs, wrapping my arms around her.

She stares up at me with her pouty lips parted, her big brown eyes filled with sadness.

I cup her jaw, running the pad of my thumb over her freckled cheeks.

"I'm sorry, Frank."

She knows I'm not apologizing just for her father's cancer, but for us too. We both know I'm partially to blame for the demise of her relationship with her parents, and it guts me to know that.

I see it in her eyes: the forgiveness, the acceptance that the past is the past.

Her hands find my hair as I drop my lips to hers. It's like she's holding me to her, not wanting me to let go.

I didn't plan on it.

Our mouths tangle together, and it's not long before we're both needing more.

Frankie is the first to pull away, resting her forehead against my shoulder.

"I thought you said no ulterior motives."

"I did, and I meant it...but I couldn't help myself."

"I'm sure you couldn't." She smiles. "How are your parents doing?"

I cough out a laugh. "Did you really just ask me how my parents are doing when I'm standing between your legs with my cock trying to bust out of my jeans?"

"Yes. Is your boner going away now? Do you still want to kiss me?"

"I always want to kiss you, Frank."

She laughs, shoving at me. "Stop it."

"No, I'm serious. I always want to kiss you. I've always *wanted* to kiss you." I take a step away and shove my hands into my pockets so I don't reach for her again. "I've kind of had a crush on you since I first saw you."

"Oh bull."

"No, I'm serious. I did. It was your first day. I saw you in the office and there was just something about you that I liked. Then we sat next to each other in first period and I was a goner."

"No." She shakes her head. "You're just saying all that to make me feel better about my crush. You didn't see me."

"Are you kidding me, Frank? You were all I saw."

"Then why didn't you ever do anything about it?"

"You were my pastor *and* my principal's daughter. I was…well, me. I couldn't touch you. We both know that."

"But you did," she murmurs, both hands placed on either side of her. "You did touch me."

"And I don't regret a single moment of it."

She doesn't say anything, just sits there swinging her legs back and forth, avoiding all eye contact with me.

"Do you?"

"Do I what, Jonas?"

She's really going to make me say it…

"Do you regret it?"

She sighs. "I've tried to." Finally, she glances up at me. "I've tried to so many times over the years."

"And?" I press.

"No, Jonas, I don't regret it."

"Good."

"Good?"

"Yeah." I grin at her. "It means I still have a chance."

Laughing, she hops down from the counter, sauntering past me, wiggling her hips in a way she knows drives me crazy.

When she reaches the doorway, she looks back at me over her shoulder with a sassy smirk.

"Wanna go make out on my couch?"

Who am I to turn her down?

I can't stay away.

I've tried.

Well, not very hard, admittedly, but I've thought hard about trying, and it's ultimately the thought that counts, right?

In between my short shifts at Slice and upping my physical therapy routine, I've shown up at Frankie's every day for the last two weeks. Sometimes it's late at night, sometimes early in the morning. Sometimes I stop by for a meal and a movie, and sometimes just for a kiss. Sometimes it's just to drop off our notebook.

I've kept her on her toes, and she's loving every second of it.

I'm about to throw her yet another curveball because I *have* to see her tonight.

I hit the green button on the phone, bringing it to my ear on an unsteady breath, suddenly nervous about making a simple phone call.

"H-Hello?"

"Frank!" My voice is too high. I'm too eager. I clear my throat. "I mean, Frank!"

Shit. Nope. That sounded exactly the same.

"Jonas?"

"Do you have many other people in your life calling you Frank? If so, I'll need names and numbers. They have some explaining to do."

"How did you get this number?"

"Julian is *very* accommodating."

"You do you realize you just made it sound like you exchanged sexual favors for my work number, right?"

"Shit. No."

She laughs. "What do you want, Jonas?"

"I want you to go to the fair with me tonight. You're not allowed to say no. Just say you'd love to go and I should pick you up at eight."

"So, basically, you're not asking me, you're telling me I'm going to the fair with you and you're picking me up at eight?"

"Yes."

"Well, then, okay. I'll see you at eight."

"Wait, seriously?" I'm surprised that worked.

"Yes." She giggles. "I mean, I'm not allowed to say no, right?"

"Right."

"Then eight it is."

"Damn, that was easy."

"Like Sunday morning."

"Hey, Frank?"

"Yeah, Jonas?"

"You're giving me twenty dollars. You're not allowed to say no."

"No."

"But I just said you can't say no."

"It doesn't work like that."

"But it just did."

"The fair thing worked because I'd actually love to go to the fair with you, but I don't want to give you twenty dollars."

"Oh, how convenient."

"Yeah—for me. See you at eight, Jonas."

Slice Ten

FRANKIE

"I'm fine, Mom, I promise. Quit fretting over me."

My mother titters on the other end of the phone. "I'm not fretting. I'm simply concerned."

"Because I have plans tonight?"

"Well...yes." *At least she doesn't lie about it.* "You never have plans."

"I do now."

She sighs, and I know exactly what's going to leave her mouth next. "Your father and I sure will miss you at dinner, Frankie."

Yep. Knew that was coming.

I'm never included in deciding when these weekly dinners will happen. I'm just supposed to keep my schedule clear and be ready when they call.

I knew dinner with them was a possibility for tonight when Jonas asked me to go to the fair with him, but I said yes anyway.

Truth is, I need a break from my parents. It's not that I don't love them, because despite everything we've gone through over the last several years and the distance that's formed between us, I still love them fiercely. It's just that they can be...overbearing. Pushy. And I have a tough time saying no to them, which never seems to end well for me.

"I'll make it up to you later this week."

"Make sure you do. I have to run now, gotta break the news to your father."

More guilt.

"I love you, Francis."

"Love you too."

I toss my phone onto the bed and meander over to my closet to continue my search for the perfect outfit.

What does one wear on a first date that hasn't actually been designated a date?

A thought hits me, and before I can overthink it, I pick my phone back up and tap Julian's name.

I already know he's going to just love getting this phone call.

"Hello?"

"I need help."

"With?"

"I need an outfit."

He sighs. "We've been over this—I am not your gay best friend who's going to give you makeovers and braid your hair and do other bullshit girly crap."

I laugh. "Except you already did give me a makeover."

"I encouraged you to do your hair and get contacts. Big whoop."

"And forced me to go to that beauty counter in the mall, and then bought me makeup."

"Okay, fine. Then we'll say I gave you a makeover. Whatever." I can practically hear him roll his eyes. "Where are you going?"

"Out."

"With?" I can picture him sitting forward, excited and eager to hear my answer because he already knows what it will be.

Julian's been walking on air since he—according to him—reunited Jonas and me.

I groan. "Stop it."

"Nah, I'm good. I want you to say it."

"Jonas," I grind out begrudgingly. "Are you happy now?"

"Delighted." He laughs like the jerk he is. "Now, where are you two lovebirds off to?"

"I'm not telling you. You'll show up."

"You really think I'm going to show up and cockblock you? After you've pined after him for years? What kind of best friend do you think I am?"

"The best of the best, Igor. And also, an asshole."

"Fair enough." He chuckles. "But I kind of need to know where you're going so I can dress you properly."

"Oh." I didn't think of that. "Fine. We're going to the county fair."

"Well this is easy: put on your shortest pair of shorts and a tight tee. Boom. Done."

"Are you serious?" I growl. "That's all you're going to say?"

"Yes, because believe it or not, dressing yourself isn't rocket science."

"Help me. Be more specific." I feel the sting of tears hit my eyes and I blink them back as fast as I can. "I don't want to screw this up, Julian."

I can hear him swallow. "Shit. Don't cry, Frankenstein. I hate it when you do that. I'm sorry. I'm taking this seriously, I promise."

"I am too, which is why it's so damn scary."

"You really like him, huh?"

"So much. I know I shouldn't because of what happened before, but I can't help it."

"Can I be honest with you?" He doesn't wait for me to answer. "Who gives a flying fuck about the past? You were kids. You did something dumb. It didn't pan out the way you wanted it to. Get over it. You're not the same person you were four years ago, and neither is he. Quit living in the past and start living in the now. You deserve it."

I don't even try to hide my tears.

He's right. About all of it. We aren't who we were before. Our lives have changed so much, and so have we. I can give him another chance and not beat myself up about it.

Maybe he'll surprise me this time around.

He has already, with the cake, the notebook, and all the times he's shown up over the last two weeks.

I just need to let go and enjoy whatever it is we're doing.

"I do, so help me pick out what to wear."

"Your dark wash shorts with the frayed hems. They make your ass look amazing. Pair it with your army green shirt with the lace on the top. It shows just enough cleavage without making you feel exposed, and it'll give Jonas something to look forward to later. And before you ask, yes, wear your gray boat shoes. They'll look just fine. I promise."

"Thank you." I blow out a breath. "You're my hero."

"I know, but just remember, you owe me."

"I promise to bring extra donuts on Monday."

"You're gonna make me wait until Monday for donuts?" he cries. "After everything I've done for you?"

"Fine. I'll let you buy me post-coitus breakfast tomorrow and rehash all the dirty details of tonight."

"Wait...seriously?"

"No!"

"Boo, you non-whore!"

"Love you, Igor."

"Love you too, Frankenstein."

Julian was right.

These shorts *do* make my ass look amazing.

"One fried Oreo for the lady."

I wrinkle my nose at the treat Jonas insisted we try. "Do I have to?"

"Where's your sense of adventure, Frank?"

I pat my pockets. "Shit. Must have left it at home."

"You left your adventure *and* your wallet at home? How convenient."

I wish I could crawl into a hole.

In my rush to get out the door and get this date going before I lost all my nerve, I completely forgot to grab my wallet.

"It wasn't on purpose, I swear!"

"That's what anyone would say."

"I'll make it up to you."

"Did you just offer sexual favors in exchange for a delicious fried cookie?"

I lift my brows. "First, I said nothing about sexual favors. Wishful thinking, much? Second, I did *not* agree to try that monstrosity of a creation."

"You're gonna turn me down now? After I spent my hard-earned money on it?

"I am ninety-five percent certain you bought that with your tip money, and considering how much pizza I've ordered in the last few weeks, there's a good chance those were my dollars."

He tries to hold back his smile at my logic but fails, and I love the way it lights up his face.

I think a smiling Jonas is my favorite thing in the world.

He holds the concoction up in front of my face. "Please?"

"Fine, but if I hate it, you owe me a funnel cake."

"Are you kidding me? That line is insane!"

"And the line for the fried Oreos wasn't. That should tell you something."

"Yeah, that everyone else in town has shitty taste."

I shake my head and snatch the fat-laden chunk from his hand, stuffing it in my mouth in one bite.

"Frank!" he shouts just as my mistake dawns on me.

It's hot.

Very hot.

My mouth is on fire and I'm doing everything I can to put it out, chewing unattractively with my mouth wide open while fanning the molten dessert.

Jonas doesn't once look at me in disgust, and not even concern.

No.

He's laughing his ass off at my mishap.

I swat at him and he doesn't care, cradling his stomach in laughter.

When I finally manage to swallow the last of the dangerous, albeit delicious, treat, I glare at him.

"You are evil!"

"How is this my fault? You're the crazy one who just grabbed and ate like she hasn't ever had a meal before."

"You could have warned me!"

"I was about to, but you just snatched it away."

"My mouth hurts. My—"

Before I can say anything else, he crashes his lips to mine and steals the breath right from my lungs.

His hands cradle my face, his thumb caressing my jaw.

It's a quick kiss, but it's packed with so much attention. So much emotion.

I loathe the moment he pulls away.

He grins at me. "Do your lips feel better now?"

"I said my *mouth* was on fire, not my lips."

"Well, in that case…"

He goes in for another kiss.

"Damn, Schwartz. Nice job." Timmy Drake, my least favorite guy from high school, whistles as he walks by. "Can't believe you bagged the virgin."

Jonas stiffens, and I see in his eyes the moment he decides he's going after Drake.

He takes one step toward the jerk, and I latch onto him, digging my heels in.

"Where do you think you're going?"

"To beat his ass," Jonas growls. "He really fucking needs it."

"Jonas…" He leans forward, and I push back. "Jonas!"

He comes to a halt, staring down at me with hard eyes.

"What?" he grinds out, and I've never heard such malice in his voice before. It almost scares me.

"What exactly do you think you're doing?"

"Well I thought it was pretty obvious I'm going to go kick that guy's ass, but apparently not." He looks down at me, eyes still full of ire. "Hey, Frank, I'm gonna go beat that guy's ass."

"You can't be serious right now."

"Oh, I'm dead serious. I'm so serious that guy is about to be dead."

"That barely makes any sense," I argue.

"I'm not trying to make sense—I'm trying to defend your honor."

"I don't need you to defend me, Jonas."

"Tell me why I'm supposed to just let him walk away after that bullshit."

"Because of your football career that's already precariously sitting on the edge of a cliff. A fight with some stupid guy who said some stupid thing that doesn't matter anyway isn't what you need right now." I shove on his chest again. "He's not worth it."

"But you're worth it, Frank. You matter."

"If I'm worth losing everything, why did you walk away last time?"

Jonas stops pushing and I stumble forward a bit.

I stare up at him, tears threatening to fall. "Why'd you leave me for the game back then? Why did you leave me, Jonas?"

I don't know where the words come from, but they're hanging between us now and I can't take them back.

He stares down at me with hurt in his eyes, like I just sucker-punched him, and I guess I did with my words.

Then his eyes flit to just about my left shoulder, and there's a sneer on his face I haven't seen before.

"Well, isn't this just perfect timing," Jonas spits.

I glance back to see who he's looking at, surprised to see my mother and father standing there.

They look so out of place at the county fair, my father in pressed dress pants and a button-up shirt, my mother wearing a pencil skirt and a dressy blouse.

"W-What are you guys doing here? I thought you were having dinner tonight."

"Well, dear," my mother starts, lips pursed in displeasure. "When we canceled, your father decided we deserved a night out for a change and took me to eat at the steakhouse across the street. We weren't quite ready to head home yet and wandered over here for some funnel cake." She glances to Jonas dismissively. "Is this the reason you couldn't make dinner with your ailing father?"

My gut fills with guilt.

"I, uh, I had a date."

"A date?" Jonas asks.

"Is this not a date?" I ask him.

"It is. I just didn't know if *you* thought it was a date. We didn't make it official or anything, but it's a date to me."

I grin. "It's a date to me too." I turn back to my parents. "Mother, Father, this is Jonas."

"We are well aware of who he is," my mother says in a tone I've never heard from her before.

It's clear she *does not* like my choice in date, and I must admit I'm shocked.

While Jonas was the quarterback of our football team, he didn't walk around like he was king, thinking he could get away with anything he wanted. He was respectful and kept up with his schoolwork. To my knowledge, he was never in the principal's office, so why my mother doesn't like him—especially since he brought nothing but glory to our old high school—I'm not sure.

"I thought I told you to stay away from my daughter."

My smile slips at the disdain I hear in my father's voice.

What the...

"How do you two know Jonas? What am I missing here?"

"I told you," Jonas says quietly. "Ask your father."

Ask your father.

His words from the night we drank ourselves dumb run through my mind.

I didn't believe him then, but I'm starting to now.

The two men shoot fire at one another with their eyes, and there is something between them I've been missing for years.

"What am I missing?" I ask again, this time directing my question solely at my father.

"Don't play dumb, Francis. You know how we know this...this...*boy*." My mother's voice drips with contempt.

"Give it up, Frank—they know."

"They know? They know what? I'm lost. I—"

Jonas raises his brows, and everything clicks into place.

They know about us, about that weekend.

"Oh," I whisper, and Jonas nods.

"Oh," he says.

What I don't understand is how that's even possible. I was careful. There was no trace of him left. I cleaned up. It was like nobody was ever there.

"H-How?" I cross my arms over my chest, shielding myself against their obvious disappointment. "How d-did you know?"

"Our notebook," Jonas tells me.

"I didn't read the entire thing," my father speaks up. "But enough to surmise that you were madly in love with this boy."

"Enough to see what he was doing to you," my mother interjects.

"Doing to me? He wasn't *doing* anything to me."

"He was leading you on just like my high school boyfriend did me, trying to change you. We had to protect you."

"Leading me on... Change me..." I laugh, but there's no humor in my voice. "Heaven forbid I step one toe out of line, that I'm not mommy's perfect princess or daddy's little angel. I am not a robot. I'm not a puppet you can manipulate, not yours to mold into whatever it is you want me to be. I am a person with my own aspirations, my own goals, my own *life*." I stomp my foot. "I make my own choices. *I* decide what school I go to. *I* decide what my career is. *I* decide who I give my virginity to and when. *I* decide who I fall in love with. It is *my* life, dammit!"

Slamming my eyes closed, I heave in a full breath for the first time in what feels like years, finally telling my parents *exactly* what I feel.

When I release it, I've never felt more relieved.

"Uh, Frank?" Jonas says tentatively.

"What?"

"I…I don't think they knew about the virginity part."

My stomach falls as I peel my eyes open.

My father's eyes are blazing. My mother is holding her hand to her chest, mouth dropped open.

They wanted me to wait until my wedding night, and not for religious reasons as many might assume with my father being a pastor.

No, my mother always told me how she regretted having sex with a man she wasn't going to marry. It was drilled into my head for years and years.

I gulp. "Oh, well, surprise…I'm not a virgin anymore."

They're hurt. They're angry.

But I'm hurt and angry too.

We stand there, squared off. It's me and Jonas against them.

He leans down, lips ghosting over my ear. "So, now the whole town definitely knows we banged."

I glance around for the first time, noticing we've managed to attract a rather large group of fairgoers.

Laughter bubbles out of me and keeps coming and coming until it eventually turns into sobs.

I look hysterical right now.

Jonas wraps his arms around me, protecting me and holding me together all at once.

"Get me out of here."

He nods, ushering me toward the exit, not stopping when my parents call after me.

He helps me into his car, dragging the seatbelt over my limp form and buckling me in safe. He presses a quick kiss to my forehead before shutting me inside and rounding the front of the vehicle.

Firing up the engine, he glances my way. "Where to?"

"Can we go to your place?"

"My parents are there. Probably still awake too."

"I don't care. I just can't go to my apartment right now. It's the first place my parents will look."

He nods, understanding. "You got it, Frank."

We pull out of the fairgrounds, speeding toward anywhere that doesn't feel like heartbreak.

Slice Eleven

JONAS

I cringe when I see the light from the TV flashing inside my childhood home as we pull up the driveway.

"What's wrong?" Frankie asks when she notices me not moving to exit the car.

"My parents are still up."

"So?"

"Well, you've never met them, so you don't really know what that means."

"Jonas, I just told half the town I'm not a virgin anymore. I think I can handle your parents just fine."

"Fine," I say, unbuckling. "But you can't say I didn't warn you."

We climb out of the car and I grab Frankie's hand as we head up the short walkway to the front door.

"You doing okay?"

We didn't talk the entire ride here. I was too afraid to bring up the debacle that just took place.

Not because I'm scared *of* Frankie, but because I'm scared *for* her.

It's clear she's in turmoil over what happened tonight.

"I'm not ready to talk about it," she says.

I respect her decision, pushing open the front door.

Aside from the noises coming from the TV, the house is otherwise quiet. I guess they just forgot to shut it off before bed.

I hold my finger up to my lips, mouthing, "*Sleeping.*" Frankie nods, and we silently make our way down the hall.

As we approach the living room, the sounds from the TV grow more audible, and I'm concerned about what my parents were watching because it's clearly sex noises.

I glance at Frankie, lifting my brows in a silent *Are you hearing this too?*

She lifts her shoulders and we press on.

I wish we hadn't.

Because on the couch are my parents.

Lips locked. Tops off. My dad's hand *clearly* up my mother's skirt.

"MY EYES!" I scream, covering my face so I can't scar myself with any other images.

"Oh shit! Letica!"

"Harvey! Grab my dress!"

There's a lot of shuffling and cussing and a whole hell of a lot of humiliation burning through me right now.

Then there's Frankie, who is standing beside me laughing so hard she's not making a sound, but I can feel her shaking.

"Knock it off," I mutter, peeking at her through my hands.

She wipes at her eyes. "Well, I just told half the town you

127

deflowered me. I guess we're square on embarrassing events to last a lifetime."

"Deflowered? Jonas Schwartz!" my mother chides. "You *deflowered* our pastor's daughter?"

I glare at her. "You were *boning* my father in the living room?"

"Actually, there was no boning. You cockblocked me," my dad helpfully explains.

I groan. "Oh my god."

"Tell me about it." My dad stands, extending a hand to Frankie. "Hi. I don't think we've ever been formally introduced. This is my wife Letica. I'm Harvey."

I smack his hand away. "Get that out of here. I don't know where that thing has been."

"Good heavens, Jonas. It's not big a deal. We've clearly had sex before."

"Twice. In my mind, you've ever only had sex twice."

My mother rolls her eyes, and my father tries not to laugh.

"Come on," I say, ignoring them and grabbing Frankie's hand. "We're going upstairs."

She laughs, giving my parents a wave as I tug her toward the staircase.

"It was great meeting you, Frankie," my father says.

"Keep the door open!" my mother hollers when we reach the top of the steps.

I roll my eyes, pushing into my bedroom and pulling Frankie inside before slamming said door closed.

I swear I hear my mother cackle.

"Look, I know I just met them, but I'm in love," Frankie says.

"They're the worst."

"Worse than your parents threatening your kind-of boyfriend away from you, making you think you did something wrong and provoking you into running and hiding for four years of your life, always pondering the what-ifs?"

I grimace.

"That's what I thought. I win."

Frankie steps around me, taking in my childhood bedroom in all its original glory.

We didn't have a lot of extra money when I was a kid, so I was surprised when I asked to repaint my room for my eighth birthday and my mother said yes. She bought the best can of paint we could afford, and we spent an afternoon together coating the walls.

Only we didn't have enough to do two coats...or the money to buy another can.

The result was a putrid green and the Power Rangers border art still peeking through.

It's an ugly room, but it's mine, and the memories attached to the remodel are some of my favorites.

I wouldn't trade it for the world.

Frankie doesn't say a word about the paint, her eyes wandering around, skimming over every small detail.

In the far corner sits my lone bookshelf that's full of everything but books.

Unless you count notebooks.

Our notebooks.

Frankie's eyes light up when she sees them, and she practically runs over, plucking one from the shelf.

She flicks through the pages, glancing over what we wrote, the things we shared, the small details of our lives that were so important back then.

There are tears in her eyes when she finally looks up at me, and I cross the room, not letting a single one trek down her cheeks.

"Don't cry."

"I can't believe you kept them."

"Of course I kept them."

"Why?"

"You think I'd throw them away?"

"I-I wasn't sure. I felt like you threw me away, so I figured…"
She trails off, her tears overwhelming her.

I pull her into me.

"I didn't throw you away, Frank. I was forced away from you.
Well, I thought I was at the time. Your father used to play football
at State. He had connections that could keep me off the team—at
least I believed he did." I squeeze her tighter. "I was wrong. I was
young and stupid, and I let the fear of losing football control me
when it should have been the fear of losing *you* that guided my
decisions."

"A part of me is glad you left," she admits quietly.

I pull back. "What? Why would you say that?"

"If you hadn't left, I'd have followed you. I would have gone to
school for something that doesn't give me the same joy football gives
you. I wouldn't have been happy in the long run."

"I wouldn't have let you follow me."

"Maybe not now, but then you would have."

I want to argue with her, but I have a feeling she's right.

"Besides, back then I was kind of enraptured by you. I wouldn't
have noticed you'd let me follow you until it was too late and I'd
already fallen out of love."

My pulse quickens.

It's the second time she's dropped the *L* word tonight, and I want
to say something about it so badly.

I want to tell her I was in love with her too.

That I never stopped being in love with her.

But I think we've had enough serious conversations for one day.

"Jonas?"

Frankie grabs my chin, stroking along my jawline and pulling my face toward hers.

"Hmm?"

Her lips ghost over mine. "Make me forget tonight."

She doesn't have to tell me twice.

I lay her on my bed and give her some new memories.

A buzzing drags me from the best night of sleep I've had in years, and I detest the thought of having to detach myself from Frankie's sleeping form.

But the moment I flip my phone over and glance at the screen, seeing my agent's name on it, I know I have to take the call.

He's been riding my ass for days now.

Which seems fair on his end, considering I was cleared for training camp last week but have been pushing off actually starting.

I was supposed to be in Colorado last night.

I never showed.

Instead, I made Frankie forget.

First with my tongue, then my fingers...then my tongue again. Finally, I buried myself inside her for what felt like hours.

Glancing over at the sleeping beauty, I carefully extract myself from her hold, using all the energy I can muster after last night, and snatch my phone from the bedside table.

"Let's get this over with," I mumble.

Frankie stirs but doesn't wake.

I hustle away, not wanting to disturb her, and slip out into the hallway, pressing dial on my agent's name.

"It's about motherfucking time, Schwartz," my agent growls into the phone. "Where the hell are you? I'm two fucking seconds from hopping on a plane and hunting your ass down."

"Would you relax, AJ? I'm still with my parents."

"That's the fucking issue! You're supposed to be in Colorado. I've had coaches blowing up my phone all goddamn morning and my wife is getting *really* tired of me taking calls when we're supposed to be on vacation."

"Please give Allie my apologies."

"Fuck your apologies, kid. I need your ass on a plane. *Now.*"

"I'm not ready yet, man."

"The contracts I have riding on your ass say you're ready. You've been dodging this for a week now. Step up to your duties or you're going to blow any chance you have at the NFL."

I sigh because I know he's right. I can't keep putting this off.

It's not that I don't want to go. I want the NFL more than anything.

But I also want Frankie.

I'm scared if I leave now, we'll never have another chance. I've lost her once and barely survived. I don't want to do it again.

"Kid?"

"Yeah, yeah," I mutter. "I'll be on a plane first thing tomorrow."

"I swear, if you dodge me again…"

"Fuck. I won't, AJ. I promise. I'll be in Colorado by noon."

"Make it before six AM?"

"Six AM? Shit." I pinch the bridge of my nose. "Okay, fine. I'll make it happen."

"I'm trusting you. Don't make me regret it."

The line goes dead, and so do all my hopes of spending more time with Frankie.

"Shit, shit, shit." I knock my head against the wall a few times, trying to rack my brain for a way to get out of this.

I don't have a solution.

The only thing I can do is be honest with Frankie about football and hope she'll understand why I have to leave again.

Carefully, I push open my bedroom door, only I don't have to be quiet.

Frankie's awake.

And from the look in her eye, she heard everything.

"You're leaving?"

I nod, and the hurt shines through just a little more.

"When were you going to tell me, Jonas?"

"I…" I run a hand through my hair. "I don't know."

She pushes up from the bed, the blanket pooling around her feet as she stands there in nothing but my old high school t-shirt and her underwear.

"When, Jonas? On the flight out of here? When you got there? You were going to tell me, right?"

The sting. The fury. The accusation that'd I'd leave and not tell her…again.

It's all there.

And it all really fucking sucks.

"Frank, I—"

"No. *No.* Don't *Frank* me. You're leaving me again. You weren't going to tell me…*again.*" She shakes her head, throwing her hands in the air. "I…I can't do this anymore. I just can't.

I rush toward her, but she puts her arms out, warding me off. She grabs her shorts off the floor and yanks them on.

"Save it. I don't want to hear it. I *can't* hear it right now, not after last night—after I stood there and told my parents you were different, that you weren't going to just lead me on. But here we are again: me giving myself to you, you taking what you want and walking away." She chokes back a sob. "I'm done with this, Jonas. I'm done with us."

Grabbing her shoes, she rushes past me.

Taking my heart right along with her.

Slice Twelve

FRANKIE

"Well, well, well. If it isn't the town hussy, the girl who let the quarterback deflower her."

Julian slides into the booth I snagged us at Ethel's Pancake Emporium.

The moment I rushed out of Jonas' house, I realized I had no way of getting back to my apartment. So, I walked to the nearest restaurant—a mile and a half away, much to my chagrin—and called Julian.

"Nice shirt." He winks at me, noting I'm still wearing Jonas' high school tee.

I groan, slinking farther down into the booth. The movement causes my shorts to rub against the beard burn between my legs just right, and I'm torn between crying and moaning at the reminder of last night.

"Shut up."

"You look…well, freshly fucked. You and Schwartz go for round two?"

That's all it takes.

The floodgates open.

"Shit, sweetie," Julian mutters, then he's crawling onto the bench beside me and wrapping his tree-trunk-sized arms around me and rubbing my back.

He lets me cry it out, not saying anything, just holding me.

I think our waiter tries to come by, but he shoos her away.

I don't know how long I stay wrapped in his embrace, but when the sobs begin to subside, he pulls my chin up, looking me over.

"Do I need to go kick his ass?"

I shake my head. "N-No, but can you kick mine for falling for his shit again?"

His brows scrunch together. "What happened?"

"He's leaving me again."

"Okay…"

"Okay?" I pull away from him. "What do you mean 'okay'?"

"What else do you want me to say? Did you not think he'd ever leave again? He's a fucking quarterback with contracts for the NFL. He was going to leave eventually."

He's not wrong. I know that, logically.

But tell it to my heart.

It sure isn't getting the message.

"I…I know that, but—"

"No. No buts, Frankie. You knew it was going to happen so you can't be upset about it."

"I can too! He left me before, Julian. This isn't the first time he's just vanished."

"The last time was bullshit and you both know it. Your

father—"

He stops, eyes widening.

How does he know...

"Julian..."

"Did I mention how drop-dead sexy you look freshly fucked?" He grabs my hair, which is loosely secured in a half-ass bun. "Your hair is to die for."

"Julian!" I smack his hand away. "Explain yourself!"

"Well, see, what happened was..."

I glare at him and he clears his throat, sitting forward.

"Fine. I ran into Jonas about six months into college. He was looking rough, and not just because he was drunk off his ass. There was just this air of sadness to him." Julian frowns as he thinks about Jonas, and it makes me frown. "Anyway, we got to talking, and before I knew it, he was crying, telling me about what your father said to him, how he had to leave you alone or give up football. I won't lie, Frankie, it really made me angry at your parents for doing that to you."

I nod. "Me too."

"Jonas tried to go after you. He was ready to abandon his dreams for you." He looks at me, almost like he's afraid to keep going. He grimaces. "But I talked him out of it."

"I—"

"For you!" he interrupts. "I did it *for* you. I knew you'd go anywhere with him, knew you'd give up your dreams of being an artist. You were just finally starting to feel free, and I didn't want you to give up your freedom. I wanted you to...well, blossom. To become *you.*" Julian covers his face with his hands. "Shit. That feels good to get off my chest."

When I don't say anything, he peeks at me through his fingers, the worry clear in his eyes.

"Are you mad?"

"No. If anything, I'm a little mad I don't make you horny."

"What the fuck?" he sputters, barely getting the words out before bursting into laughter. "What the hell, Frankie?"

"Look"—I lift a shoulder—"I'm just saying, it's a shame we never banged. I feel like I owe you after you did me that favor."

He lifts his brows. "You're really not mad?"

"I'm really not. In fact, I said almost the same thing to Jonas last night. Don't get me wrong, I was furious at him for leaving me, for hurting me, but the more I look back on it, the more grateful I am. In a roundabout way that wasn't about me at all, he helped me."

"Well shit, now I do have a boner."

I roll my eyes. "Move back to your side before I punch you."

"Fine, but I want to hear more about last night. Please tell me that beard of his feels as good as it looks."

"What am I supposed to do, Julian?" I ask once he's settled across from me.

"Um, ride the beard again. How is that even a question?"

"You know damn well that's not what I'm talking about."

"Yeah, yeah." He pouts, crossing his arms over his chest. "You always find a way to ruin all the fun girl talk with your stupid feelings."

I pick up the menu, perusing it. "You're paying for your own breakfast now."

"I most certainly am not."

"That's where you're wrong. I don't have my wallet."

"Well you better get your hussy ass back to the kitchen and get to work on some sad hand jobs to earn some money. It's your turn to pay."

"Sad hand jobs? Really, Julian?" I groan. "I am about to strangle you, and that is *not* how I want to start my day."

"I have a bold suggestion for you," he says, ignoring my empty threats. "How about you talk to Jonas like a grown-ass adult?"

"He's already leaving—there's no need to talk to him. It's not like I can ask him to put his football career on hold for me so we can chitchat about our feelings."

"When is he leaving?"

"He has to be in Colorado by tomorrow morning."

"So talk to him now."

"I am *not* showing up at his house after storming out this morning. That is so not in the cards. I also need to avoid my apartment for at least another few hours so my parents will quit staking it out."

He cringes. "Things were that bad last night?"

"Awful. I'll talk to them eventually, but I need time…kind of like I need time with Jonas."

"But you don't have time."

"I know this, Julian." I sigh, folding my menu and glaring at him. "I know I don't. I love him and I don't have time to tell him. I don't have time to show him, but just let me handle this, okay?"

He eyes me, not saying anything but saying everything all at once.

He doesn't trust me to talk to Jonas.

And to be fair, I don't either.

I've become really good at avoiding all things Jonas over the years. I buried my love for him before, so maybe I can do it again.

"I *will* handle it, all right?"

"Right. Fine. Whatever."

"Whatever," I mimic.

I pick my menu back up, propping it up on the table, blocking my best friend from my line of sight.

He does the same.

We don't speak for several minutes, each only pretending to examine the menu because we've been here dozens of times and always get the same thing.

"Tell you what, since I'm in a giving mood this morning, I'll split the hand jobs with you. You hit the waitstaff and I'll get the guys in the back. Deal, Frankenstein?"

I can't help it—a giggle bursts out of me because my best friend is a moron, and the icy war is over.

"Deal, Igor."

"Good gravy, I'm coming!"

I pull myself off the couch for the first time in what feels like days. It's only been a few hours, but Netflix has judged me at least three times.

"What?" I growl, throwing the door open.

I'm met with a sight I didn't expect: Brad, the delivery guy from Slice.

"W-What are you doing here, Brad?"

"I, uh, had a delivery for here."

"But I didn't order anything. Are you sure?"

"I've delivered to this address many times." He grins but humors me and checks the receipt in his hand. "I'm certain this is you."

"Well, I still didn't order anything."

"I mean, it's already been paid for, so you might as well take the free pie, Miss Callahan."

"Fine." I take the box he's holding out in front of him. "Let me grab you a five."

"I've been tipped already, miss."

My brows shoot up. "What?"

He waves the receipt. "All taken care of. Have a great night, Miss Callahan."

I'm stricken. What the hell is happening? I didn't order a pizza. As good as it sounds, I'm too upset to eat right now. I barely even touched my favorite strawberry pancakes at Ethel's this morning.

Brad is halfway down the hall before I compose myself enough to speak.

"Who sent it?"

He shoots me a mischievous grin. "That's confidential."

I blink back at him, and he spins on his heel, hustling out the door without giving me an answer.

What in the world…

I take a glance around, half wondering if I've been put on some sort of weird reality prank show or if I'm just going insane.

But nobody is here filming.

I must be going insane.

I back inside my apartment, closing my door, staring at it like it might explode.

Nothing happens.

"Well, let's see what I got," I say, making my way back to my couch.

I flip open the lid, and the first thing I notice is the mouthwatering pizza.

Even though I wasn't hungry before, I'm starved now.

I grab a slice as I throw open the box the rest of the way.

"Come to mama." I've shoved nearly half a slice into my mouth when something catches my eye.

Scrawled on the lid of the box in handwriting I know all too well is a note.

I'm sorry.

Not for the pizza, but for everything else.

Everything except loving you.

He *loves* me?

Jonas...loves *me?*

I spring to my feet, racing toward the door, hoping and praying I can catch Brad before he leaves because I *have* to make sure I'm not going crazy and this is really happening.

Swinging open the door, I immediately crash into a brick wall...or Jonas. They feel like the same thing at this point.

He grabs me by the shoulders, righting me.

His simple touch does me in, my knees trying to buckle. Shock courses through me, and so many emotions flying around inside me.

The most notable sensation is relief, because Jonas is here, which means he's not ready to give up on us.

Neither am I.

"What are you doing here? You should be on a flight."

"I have exactly one hour. Leroy's waiting for me in the parking lot." He rocks back on his heels, giving me a hopeful look. "Can we talk?"

"Make it quick."

He stumbles back. "Frank, I—"

"I lied. We can't talk."

"We...we can't?"

"No, because I don't want to spend our last hour together talking. I want to spend it kissing. I want to spend it in your arms."

He moves with a speed I've never seen before, his hands crashing through my hair as he pulls me into him, lifting me by my ass and shoving me against the nearest wall. His mouth slams down on mine with such force it almost hurts.

"Fuck, Frank." He exhales against my lips. "You had me scared for a minute."

He presses his mouth to mine again, kissing me long and hard, stealing the breath straight from my lungs.

"I love you," I confess, pulling away, breathing like I just ran a marathon. "I love you too. I've always loved you, even when I was mad at you."

"I'm so sorry." Kiss. "For everything." Kiss. "I want to take it all back and do it all over again all at the same time."

"I know, I know."

I kiss him again, loving the feel of his beard scraping against my chin.

I don't know how long we stay there tangled in one another, but I know I never want it to end.

"Your knee," I say during one of our short breaks. "Isn't this killing your knee?"

"No. Your kisses healed me."

Laughing, I shove at him, wiggling free and planting my legs back on the floor.

He has one arm slung above me, and he's staring down at me with hunger in his gaze as his fingers play along my skin where my shirt has ridden up. I love the feel of his hands on me. I'm going to miss it.

The reality of him leaving any minute hits me, and I work to blink back tears, my lips quivering.

I crash into his chest, and he lets me cry it out.

"Hey," he says softly after several minutes. "No more crying, Frank. I gotta leave in five minutes. I don't want you to cry."

"How can I not cry? You're going to be all the way in Colorado, and I'll be here in North Carolina. I can't leave. My dad is sick. It doesn't matter how angry I am at him…I can't leave, and you know that. What are we going to do, Jonas? How are we going to make this work?"

"I don't know, but I know we can." He pulls my chin up toward his face, so much determination in his eyes. "We can do this."

"How? Where do we start?"

"It's just like a game of football, baby. You be the home team and

I'll be the visitor. We'll take turns on each other's turf. It's not gonna be perfect. It'll be messy as hell, but we're gonna give each game our all, leaving it all out on the field. It's all we can do."

"What if we lose?" I ask.

"Then at least we'll have played the game."

Another tear falls, and he's quick to wipe it away.

He brings his lips to mine again, and I know it's the last time our mouths will touch today.

"I have to go," he whispers, pulling away.

"I know." I nod. "I know. We'll be good. We'll be fine."

"We will," he promises, backing away. "We can make this work. We'll play the game."

"Give it our all," I agree as he twists the knob on the door.

"Will you write to me? In our notebook? I mean, we can still text and call and all that other fancy crap they have these days, but can we still use that too?"

"Like mail it back and forth?"

"Yeah. I mean, I know it's a bit silly, but it just seems too important of a tradition to let go."

"I'll write to you. I'll start tonight."

He nods, giving me a sad smile, looking at me like the last thing he wants to do is leave.

I feel the same way.

"I really have to go now," he says reluctantly.

"I know." I sniffle, wiping away an errant tear. "Go. I'll be fine."

"Are you sure?"

"I'm sure. Promise."

"I'll call you as soon as I land."

I swallow the lump in my throat, bobbing my head up and down.

"Bye Frank," he whispers.

The door clicks shut behind him, the sound thunderous as I

choke back a sob.

We're doing this. We're playing the game. We can make it work this time. We're not kids anymore. We're not living under someone else's rules.

We can do this.

I didn't say I love you.

The thought slams into me, and I *have* to say it. I *need* to tell him.

I pull open the door, ready to race down the hall after him, but I stop short of running smack into Jonas for a second time.

"I love you!" I blurt.

He laughs, hauling me into his arms again. "I know you do, Frank. I know."

I bury my face in his neck, inhaling the scent that's purely him, committing it to memory.

"Meet me at the 50-yard line?" he whispers.

"I'm already there waiting for you."

A Slice of the Future

FRANKIE

JONAS: Missing you bad tonight. I'm sorry I can't be there for our one-year anniversary. Should have planned this shit better.

ME: Yeah you should have.

JONAS: Hey! You're supposed say you miss me too.

ME: You know I do.

JONAS: How much? Like read our notebook kind of much? You've been saving it for tonight, haven't you?

ME: How'd you know?

JONAS: Because you never commented on any of my witty anecdotes. And because you always save them for nights you'll need them.

ME: Whatever. I'm starting it now, so hush.

JONAS: How are you so sassy from so far away?

ME: It's a gift. Now zip it.

JONAS: Yes ma'am!

I smile down at my phone.

I haven't seen Jonas in three weeks now, and somehow, it feels like a lifetime.

Stupid when you consider the fact that we once went four years without each other.

Since he left for Colorado last year to start his career, we've made a point to see each other at least every other month. It's a little hectic to schedule—and a little heavy on my budget—but we do it anyway because we can't seem to get enough of each other.

Each time Jonas shows up on a Friday and leaves on a Sunday, he drops our notebook onto my hallway table just before he leaves, and each time, I save it for a day when I'll really need it.

Like tonight. Our one-year anniversary.

I still can't believe we've been together for a whole year now, let alone the fact that we've spent all of it doing the long-distance thing.

But that's coming to an end soon. I hope.

My dad is doing a lot better than he was. He even got to ring the bell three months ago.

I would have jumped on a plane to be with Jonas that day, but I was offered a promotion at work that I couldn't pass up.

We decided we'd wait until the season is over to figure out what our next move is in terms of being together full-time.

I won't lie, the wait is excruciating.

The irrational part of my brain says to just quit my job and jump in with both feet.

The rational part knows that's a stupid idea.

And it's not like Jonas can just move wherever he pleases with his budding NFL career.

So we wait.

We wait and it sucks.

It sucks because we keep missing things, like birthdays. Some holidays. Anniversaries.

On a sad sigh, I open our latest notebook—we're on our sixth for the year—flipping through the pages, smiling at the silly things we tend to write to each other.

I stop at one I both love and hate to read, because apparently I'm a glutton for punishment.

Yesterday at practice the guys were talking about all the dates they've been scoring on Tinder. I won't lie, it makes me super fucking jealous. I want to take you on dates. I want to go home to you at night, not an apartment full of horny jocks. I want your goodnight kisses and your good morning ones too.

I want you.

God, I fucking miss you.

Shit. Sorry.

I shouldn't have written that. That's not going to be fun for you to read later.

I'm sorry.

I love you.

My heart tugs at the ache I feel in his words.

Jonas apologized to me for that before I even read it.

I'm glad I had some warning, because if I'd have read that without one, I'd have broken.

I flip the page, hoping for something funny to follow.

Remember the dude I told you about who thinks he's hot shit?
Guess who shit his pants in the gym today in front of everyone...
Instant. Fucking. Classic.

We laughed about that one for weeks.

The guy deserved it, especially after he sacked Jonas in practice. Jerk.

I flip through to another page.

We have a video chat scheduled in five minutes, but I had to get this off my chest before I explode and accidentally tell you.

Remember last week when we were discussing some of our sexual fantasies?

One of mine is watching you get off with a toy that I control.

Today, I ordered you a vibrator.

You don't know this yet because it won't get there until tomorrow.

So that means you also don't know that I had the controller sent here.

Fuck, I can picture you blushing while reading this, and it has my dick aching.

Shit. Now I'm hard and you're calling and I'm not asking for another video chat until you have that vibrator.

So just remember when you're reading this later, I had a boner the entire time we talked.

I'm pathetic.

Jonas isn't here and he's causing me to ache.

When his gift arrived, I almost didn't open it because I knew I hadn't ordered anything.

He was right—I did blush when I saw the toy.

Then I used it…without him.

I couldn't stop myself.

I pulled it right out of the package, charged it, and took it for a spin.

And what a spin it was.

Jonas did good. Jonas did *real* good.

If possible, it was even better having him control it from a thousand miles away. It's been a steady star of our video chats lately, especially the longer we stay separated.

I flip the page again, hoping for something that'll make me laugh and *not* think about missing him.

Roses are red.
I don't believe violets are blue.
I miss Slice pizza.
Just like I miss you.

He wrote that poem—if it can even be called that—last month, just two days before he flew out. He walked into my apartment, Slice box in hand, two slices missing.

I teased him for it and then informed him violets are in fact blue.

We argued about it until we fell into bed together.

And now I'm thinking about Jonas naked again.

Maybe flipping through our notebooks when my vibrator needs a charge isn't the best idea…

I turn the page anyway, excited because whatever I read next is going to be new.

I like to save the new material as long as I can, only allowing myself the treats on days I'm really missing Jonas.

*Do me a favor, **will** you?*
Draw more pictures for me. Like you used to back in high school.
I need something new to hang in my locker.

I was thinking about your ankles the other day.
I know, I know. It sounds nuts.
*But remember that time I told you I bet **you** had sexy ankles?*
I was right.
Also, I ate an orange today just because I missed you.
Stop judging me.

I was craving frozen yogurt tonight and went to a place just down the street.
It reminded me of our first weekend together and all those damn sundaes you made us eat because you went overboard with the junk food.
I didn't eat ice cream for years after that. It made me sad just to think about it.
*I love ice cream again now, and memories of that weekend make me all **marry** and shit.*
I don't think you can say "and shit" at the end of a statement like that and it still be romantic, but we're going with it. No takebacks and all that.
I love you, Frank.

Of course Jonas would find a way to make me smile over the use of the word shit.

Someone should probably talk to him about his spelling though, because that's definitely *not* the version of merry he intended to use.

I wet my finger and turn the page, kind of loving how sentimental he's getting over our history.

I never thought you'd give me another chance after everything went down with us all those years ago.

I'm so fucking glad you did.

It was the beard, wasn't it?

Either way, you make **me** *feel like the luckiest son of a bitch in the whole world.*

I love you, Frank.

Always have, always will, baby.

How is it possible he can take my breath away from across the country?

I flip the page again, and my brows instantly slam together.

Well, what's the answer? You're killing me here.

Answer? To what question?

Did he mean to write that?

I think back to the phone conversations we've had, trying to figure out if he asked me a question I never gave him an answer for, if this is some inside joke I'm just not picking up on right now.

I'm coming up blank.

I go back through the most recent notes, and I can't find any unanswered questions in them either.

Then something catches my eye.

"What the hell…" I mutter, staring down at the words sticking out at me. "No. There's no way…"

I shake my head, smiling as my heart begins to swell, tears prickling my eyes from the emotional overload I'm experiencing.

Right there, in bolded letters, it reads, *Will you marry me?*

I laugh, and the tears fall free.

That's why he used marry and not merry.

I grab my phone to call him just as the doorbell chimes through my tiny apartment, signaling the arrival of my dinner.

I figured if I couldn't spend my anniversary with my main squeeze, I'd go for my second love—pizza.

Crossing my small living room, I swipe at the happy tears rolling down my cheeks and smooth down my hair, trying to look like less of a mess for the poor delivery person on the other side of the door.

"It's about goddamn time," I hear when I pull it open.

My knees almost buckle, and my hand goes straight to my chest, trying to hold my leaping heart inside. "Jesus!"

"No. My name is Jonas. Like the Weezer song."

I stare at him, mouth hanging open.

Somehow, even though I only saw him three weeks ago, he looks bigger, bulkier. He looks every bit the NFL quarterback that he is.

And *that beard.*

I bite my lip just thinking about the way it feels between my legs. Snapping out of it, I launch myself into his arms.

He catches me like he was made to do just that.

"I can't believe you're here!" I say into his neck, because that's where my face is buried. "Wait." I pull back. "*How* are you here?"

"Well, this may come as a shock to you, but in 1903, right here in North Carolina, they built this thing called an airplane and—*ow!* What the hell, Frank? Quit pulling my hair."

"Quit being a smartass and kiss me."

He does.

Jonas crashes his mouth against mine, capturing my lips in a kiss that steals my breath and breathes life into me all at the same time. His hard lips move against mine, fitting over them like they were made for kissing me.

When we pull apart after what feels like hours and all too soon, he grins at me.

His full lips pull into a smirk. "Hey, Frank."

"Hi. I missed you."

"I missed you more."

"Liar."

"I flew like 1,800 miles just to kiss you—I definitely miss you more."

"Just to kiss me, huh?"

"Well, to kiss you and to see those sexy ankles of yours."

I laugh, pressing a kiss to his lips because I can't help myself.

"So, Frank," he says when he pulls away. "Did you, uh, happen to get through all my notes?"

"I did."

"Yeah? Read anything interesting?"

"I did, actually. I read that you have a thing for fro-yo."

"God, I hate that word. Fro-yo sounds so stupid."

I continue like he didn't interrupt me. "You eat oranges when you miss me, and you definitely *do* fantasize about my ankles."

"I warned you before..."

I grin. "You did, yet I fell for you anyway."

"That's your own fault then."

"I'll gladly accept that fault of mine."

"Come across anything else in those notes?"

"Hmm." I twist my lips, tilting my head, pretending to think. "Nothing comes to mind."

"I'm starting to regret coming home."

"Liar," I say against his neck, nipping at the soft skin.

"Frank..." He throws his head back on a groan, but I can't tell if it's because he's tired of my teasing or the nip. "You're killing me."

"Sexually? Or because I won't answer you?"

"Yes." The word is pushed out through gritted teeth.

I laugh. "Okay, fine. But first, I have a request."

"Name it. It's yours."

"Dibs on Julian to be my maid of honor."

154

"Done, but I call Thea for best man."

"Oh, man. She's gonna be *so* annoyed she has to get a date for the wedding."

"She'll get over it." He shrugs. "Besides, I'm sure she'll find some poor unlucky victim to take mercy on her."

"I guess we'll see."

"Is that your way of saying yes?"

I purse my lips. "What was the question again?"

He tightens his grip on my ass, squeezing me hard but not hard enough to hurt. "I'll drop you right here in the middle of this hallway..." he threatens, loosening his grip enough for me to slip a couple inches.

I strengthen my hold on him, pulling myself back up his body. "You most certainly will not."

"Oh, I will. I'll do it."

"Weird. I will too."

His brows scrunch together. "What?"

I roll my eyes. "I will, Jonas. I'll marry you. I'll meet you at the 50-yard line."

Slowly, a grin curves his mouth up. "Yeah?"

"Definitely."

"Thank god, Frank." He drops his forehead against mine, lips hovering right over my own. "Because I've been waiting to make you mine for far too long."

Other Titles by Teagan Hunter:

Want to be part of a fun reader group, gain access to exclusive content and giveaways, and get to know me a little more?
Join Teagan's Tidbits on Facebook!

Want to stay on top of my new releases?
Sign up for New Release Alerts!

TEAGAN HUNTER is a Missouri-raised gal, but currently lives in South Carolina with her Marine veteran husband, where she spends her days begging him for a cat. She survives off coffee, pizza, and sarcasm. When she's not writing, you can find her binge-watching various TV shows, especially *Supernatural* and *One Tree Hill*. She enjoys cold weather, buys more paperbacks than she'll ever read, and never says no to brownies.

You can find Teagan on Facebook:
https://www.facebook.com/teaganhunterwrites

Instagram:
https://www.instagram.com/teaganhunterwrites

Twitter:
https://twitter.com/THunterWrites

Her website:
http://teaganhunterwrites.com

Or contact her via email:
teaganhunterwrites@gmail.com

Gloucester Library
P.O. Box 2380
Gloucester, VA 23061

CPSIA information can be obtained
at www.ICGtesting.com
Printed in the USA
LVHW091123250620
658806LV00011BA/1556

9 798637 487813